JERRY SCOTT and
JIM BORGMAN

Zits

SHREDDED

HARPER TEEN

An Imprint of HarperCollinsPublishers

HarperTeen is an imprint of HarperCollins Publishers.

Zits: Shredded
Copyright © 2014 by Jerry Scott and Jim Borgman
All rights reserved. Printed in the United States of America.
No part of this book may be used or reproduced in any manner whatsoever without
written permission except in the case of brief quotations embodied in critical articles
and reviews. For information address HarperCollins Children's Books, a division of
HarperCollins Publishers, 10 East 53rd Street, New York, NY 10022.
www.epicreads.com

Library of Congress catalog card number: 2013953797
ISBN 978-0-06-222853-6

14 15 16 17 18 CG/RRDH 10 9 8 7 6 5 4 3 2 1

First Edition

For the King Features folks, who go
the extra mile for us day after day after day:
Rocky Shepard, Keith McCloat, Brendan Burford,
Frank Caruso, Claudia Smith, John Killian, Richard
Heimlich, Jack Walsh, Dennis Danko, Lou Albert,
Mike Mancino, Robin Graham, John Perry,
and Evelyn Smith

CHAPTER 1

That's the trouble with milking french fries—slippery elbows. Once you've been at it for a couple of hours, you get a grease slick down your forearms that threatens your stability. One careless bump from, say, your 230-pound sumo-size best friend and you can go skidding forward across the table, sending a giant cup of your morning's work sliding ahead of you. As in just now. We all freeze as the oily Big Slurp teeters on the edge, and then dumps about seventeen fossil fuel–free miles onto the floor and into the crisp cuffs of some salesman's khakis.

Ever since we had the van converted to run on veggie oil,

Hector, Pierce, and I have been scrounging stray fries and orphan onion rings off abandoned fast-food trays and squeezing the free mileage out of them. It's annoyingly slow, and even if we're careful we can't get more than a cup of grease out of a small order of fries. There are sixteen cups in a gallon, and the van has a ten-gallon tank. Do the math. There's no way I'm wasting this puddle of liquid freedom.

"Don't just sit there," I yell. "SCOOP!" Pierce dives for the floor, and Hector grabs a spare cup while I try to surround the pool of oil that's spreading slowly across the table.

Before long, we salvage most of the spill, and I carefully snap a plastic lid on the cup. Out of the corner of my eye, I see the salesman guy flipping us off on his way out the door.

"What's his problem?" I ask.

"No idea," says Pierce. "Dude was slapping at me with the comics section the whole time I was under his table. Talk about anger issues!"

Hector scrolls through the apps on his phone, and then taps the maps icon. He sits up really straight and gets this weird, plastic look on his face.

"Contestants," he rumbles in a deep, corny announcer voice. "The category is Historic Cool Places We Should Visit."

"Can we just have a normal conversation for once?" Pierce moans. "As in, *If you were going to get a Renaissance painting tattooed on the roof of your mouth, what would it be?*"

Ignoring him, Hector goes on. "This band famously played a nineteen-hour jam at the Pioneer Inn in Nederland, Colorado, that launched their career. You have five seconds." Then he starts to hum that *Jeopardy* tune. Hector's game-show host imitation always cracks me up. I hate that buzzer of his, though.

"Does anybody have a guess?" Hector prides himself on his obscure

rock trivia, and he totally thinks he has me stumped. I fan the air and raise my hand.

"Who is the String Cheese Incident? Duh. Does anybody not know that?" Hector slumps back down to his normal posture and mumbles something in Spanish. He hates it when I get these answers right.

"AARGH! I knew that one," Pierce howls and then pops a mutant onion ring in his mouth. A half second later he remembers where we found those onion rings.

"Dude! Keep your head in the game! That's free fuel you're wasting," I yell.

"Sorry . . . sorry," he mumbles as he wipes his tongue on his T-shirt, then wrings his T-shirt into the cup. Then we all get back to the business of milking french fries.

Converting the van to run on veggie oil has been kind of a hassle, to tell you the truth. It all started when Sara came back from an OSSWRAC (Overly Strident Students World Resource Austerity Conference) in Columbus last fall. She was all hyped up about stuff like eliminating fossil fuels and stopping global warming. I was picking her up after band practice when out of nowhere she gets this amazing idea:

Who knows what inspires these insights? At the time, it seemed like an awesomely excellent suggestion, but let's face it, almost any suggestion is awesomely excellent when the suggester is a hot girl wearing skinny jeans, boots, and a tight tank top. I mentioned it to Hector, who mentioned it to Pierce, who called his uncle, the motorcycle mechanic, who happened to know everything there is to know about converting diesel engines to run on veggie oil. He got his automotive training at an ashram in Bhutan, so he's a master of reincarnated engines. And he knows his yaks, too.

There were a couple of problems to overcome right away, like the fact that the van didn't have a diesel engine and it was going to cost *way* more than we could afford. But Pierce's mom stepped in and traded Pierce's uncle the bail money he still owed her for the cost of converting the van. We even got to help with the conversion, which we all found educational.

After about a hundred trips to the junkyard and a month of weekends, we actually got the van's new used diesel engine running on recycled veggie oil. And even though it can be kind of a pain to scrounge for used grease, the van is more awesome than ever because (1) it's überly good for the planet (the van's old motor put enough CO_2 in the atmosphere to melt an iceberg),

(2) it's a total chick magnet,

and (3) it always smells like french fries.

Combine that with the fact that the fuel is basically free and available in any fast-food Dumpster or alley and you have a win-win-win-win situation.

I squeegee another drop of oil into a fresh cup and catch a glimpse of Hector tapping on his phone screen again. We've been working out the route of our Epic Summer Road Trip since we bought the van. The plan is to take off the day after we graduate and spend the summer rolling down the highway on good karma and fast-food squeezings. Yeah, okay, it's still a ways off, but a journey of this magnitude takes serious planning. Hector switches off his calculator app and announces, "At twenty-five miles per gallon, the String Cheese detour to Colorado would take just over forty-nine gallons of grease."

"Totally agree," I say. "Add it to the itinerary." And then we all groan as a big jock at the next table downs two huge fistfuls of fries whose partially hydrogenated innards would have gotten us halfway to St. Louis.

"Let's get back to Midwest destinations," suggests Hector. He holds his phone up for Pierce and me to see. "I think it's pretty clear that there's nothing really interesting between Moline, Illinois (the birthplace of three of the founding members of Flatulent Rat), and Hibbing, Minnesota (the boyhood home of Bob Dylan), agreed?"

"Just Chicago," shrugs Pierce.

"Right. So it only makes sense that we'd head west from Hibbing and drive straight through to Jamestown, North Dakota."

"Correct," says Hector. "And the next logical stop would be . . . ?"

"Jerome, Arizona, home of the world's best buffalo-wing restaurant," I answer, channeling his brain.

"I love it when a plan comes together," Hector says, topping off another cup of grease. Then something outside catches my eye. Climbing over Hector and standing on the back of his chair is the only way I can really see through the giant dancing cheeseburger that's covering most of the window. I'm no advertising expert, but does this restaurant really believe that an anthropomorphic sandwich with a top hat is going to make me hungrier? Doubtful.

Anyway, by lining my head up just right to look through the cheeseburger's monocle I can see Sara's tan 2005 Sensible Boringmobile ease into a spot at the far end of the parking lot. She says that she likes to park in the very last space because there's less chance of her car doors getting dented, but I think it's because her car is so incredibly bland that it's the only way she can find it later.

"Sara, D'ijon, and Autumn just pulled in," I report, scrambling back over Hector's shoulders.

"Are they coming in here?" Pierce asks as we all grab for our phones.

After a quick look-check, we try to think of a way to seem all casual and bored. It's important that a guy never appear eager or needy in front of females; they can smell pathetic a mile away. So we all get ourselves arranged in our best fake kick-back poses right as the girls roll in the door. Sara looks around the restaurant, points at us, and then they all stroll over to our totally relaxed corner. The element of cool is on our side.

Okay . . . WAS on our side.

CHAPTER 2

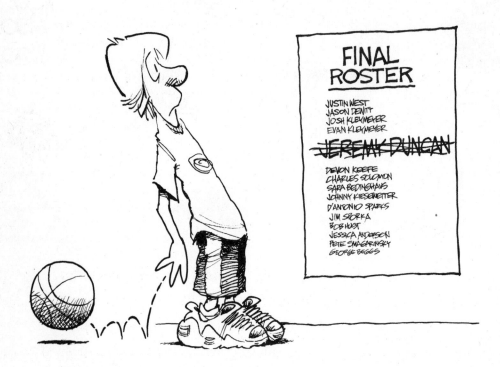

FINAL ROSTER

JUSTIN WEST
JASON DEWITT
JOSH KLEYMEYER
EVAN KLEYMEYER

~~JEREMY DUNCAN~~

DEVON KEEFE
CHARLES SOLOMON
SARA BEDINGHAUS
JOHNNY KIESENETTER
D'ANTONIO SPARKS
JIM SPORKA
BOB HUGT
JESSICA ANDERSON
PETE SMAGARINSKY
GEORGE BEGGS

*D*umped. Yeah, not my favorite word. When I was in the fifth grade, I was the only one out of the fifteen kids who tried out for basketball that didn't make the team. The official reason was that they only had fourteen team uniforms, but it felt more like being dumped. I think the whole thing would have blown over fairly quickly if the coach hadn't tried to make it all better by naming me Head Male Cheerleader as a consolation prize. Thanks for the popularity boost, Coach! I spent the whole basketball season faking laryngitis and forging excuse notes from my mom. To this day I get queasy at the sight of a pom-pom.

"*Dumped* is a strong word," I squeak, bracing myself for the millionth discussion with Sara about us. She seems to easily surf the waves of relationship junk between us, while I get caught in every boy-girl riptide and undertow there is. I guess that putting up with these emotional slogathons every few weeks is the price a horndog like me pays to keep my name in the same sentence with a hot girl like Sara. But as I mentally line up my usual set of all-purpose apologies and peace offerings, I realize something isn't adding up. This was a *mass* dumping? Did these three just get picked up by a roving band of triplets in the parking lot?

"You're right, I need a stronger word," she says. "How about *rejected*? Or *burned*?"

Then D'ijon jumps in to put a point on it.

YOU GUYS JUST GOT TOSSED OFF A THOUSAND-FOOT CLIFF INTO A FLAMING DUMPSTER FULL OF CLOWNS WITH RAZORS!

For a few seconds Pierce, Hector, and I don't say anything while that image sets up camp in our brains. When the silence lasts too long and Sara can see that our minds have wandered, she herds them back to reality with a little clarification.

CONNOR MATTSON JUST HIRED A DJ FROM COLUMBUS! GOAT CHEESE PIZZA WILL **NOT** BE PLAYING HIS BIRTHDAY PARTY GIG.

Oh. That. Whew.

For those who haven't heard, or may be living in a cave somewhere without Wi-Fi or a decent smartphone, Connor Mattson throws the best party of the year, every year. Period. The dude's birthdays are epic for two reasons: his parents, who are never there. We actually got to play a set at his last party, back when we were still calling ourselves Chickenfist, and we were happy to grovel for the chance. Mattson never respected us, I could tell, but he was desperate because his usual band, Lung Mustard, was breaking up over "creative differences." (The creative differences happened when their bass player's mom read the explicit version of the lyrics to his newest song, "Exacerbation." They say that she backed her minivan over his amp and donated his guitar to the PTA's Monkees cover band. The poor guy is now playing clarinet in the marching band and spending the rest of his time collecting socks for the homeless.)

Mattson acted all grateful when we said yes and then air-penciled us in for the party next month, but I always wondered if he really meant it. Whatever. Goat Cheese Pizza remains dumped and that causes a serious crapification of everyone's mood. Then Sara cheers us down even further by suddenly changing the subject to college application deadlines. I swear, this girl's brain cells ping around like a handful of marbles in a food processor. I don't feel like talking about anything having to do with school, so I grab her hand and climb over Hector.

"I need some air. Let's drive." Hector and Pierce grab the three cups of french fry grease we've collected and we all head for the van. I get there first, automatically making me the driver. Pierce and Hector funnel the precious oil into the fuel tank while I hold the doors open for the girls. Two minutes and eleven conversations later, we're rolling.

As usual, everybody ignores me, so I do what I always do and just free-style it. There's nothing like driving, especially when there are other people in the car. With the (obvious) exception of my mom, I like to listen to people talk when I'm behind the wheel and just get lost in the experience. Not lost like Pierce-lost (the guy has an epically bad sense of direction), but just living in the moment.

"Hello? Can we get back to the college applications?" D'ijon is pretty intense when it comes to her education, and a collective groan circulates through the van when she asks, "Is anybody besides me worried about this community service project requirement?"

I make a right turn because right turns tend to make the

engine run a little better. Pierce says that he's going to figure out why that happens, but it doesn't really bother me too much. I'm good at right turns, so maybe it's just one of those things that's meant to be, you know?

D'ijon has everybody's attention, so she keeps rolling. "Okay, first of all? I do NOT think it's fair that the rest of us have to compete with people like Gilbert or Phoebe." We all mutter in agreement. "I mean, those people have been geeking out on service and charity projects since they were in elementary school. Their extracurricular activities résumés would make Gandhi look like a slacker!

CHILL, PLEASE! I AM PLAYING GRAND THEFT AUTO 5!

Does that sound like a level playing field to you?"
"Well, it—" starts Hector.

The thing you need to know about D'ijon is that when she asks a question, she pretty much has the answer she wants in her head already. Coming up with your own is not always a great idea.

"The answer is no because the rest of us have not had the opportunity to focus on others because we have been busy creating the selves we have become. Do I hear an amen?"

BBBLA
BBBLMN

After two awkward seconds, D'ijon is calmed down and I'm hearing talk about nail color, fart quality, and what's good this week on Hulu. That's more like it.

But the more I think about it, D'ijon has a point. And it's clear to me that the only way any of us are going to get into a good college is if the girls take on some crazy-ambitious public-service project and let us guys pretend to help. Everybody knows that group projects only have a chance at succeeding if and only if there's at least one girl on the team; it's a scientific fact, like gravity or yetis.

My phone buzzes with a text, so I hand it to Sara to read, which she does with a dead-on impression of my mom.

There's a chorus of awwws! and Isn't that sweets!, but I don't care. I'm starving, and happy to see that we're basically back where we started. I yank the van into the space next to Sara's car, and the girls pile out in a tumble of tight jeans, air-kisses, and good-byes. Hector resumes his usual shotgun position, Pierce lays down a rhythm on what's left of the van's headliner, and I order a double bacon jalapeño cheeseburger in the drive-thru lane in case my mom's serving vegetarian or anything smaller than an alpaca. Dinnertime, here I come!

If there's one thing in my life that's certain, it's that my dad never yells. Well, there was that time when he tried to take a shower after me and had to wait forty-five minutes for hot water.

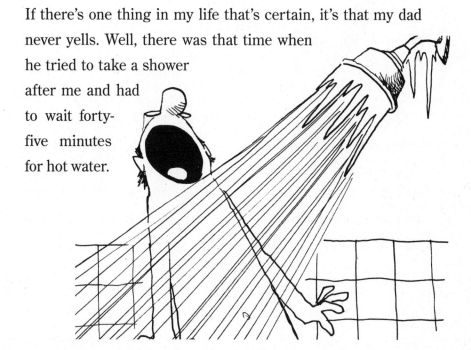

And once he was helping me back in to the garage and I ran over his foot, and . . .

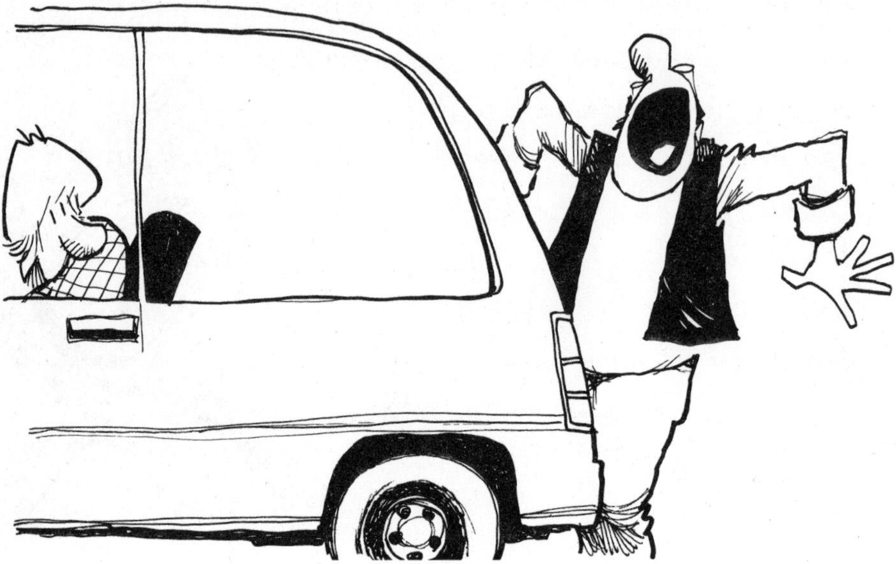

. . . Oh, wow. Now that I think about it, my dad yells all the time.

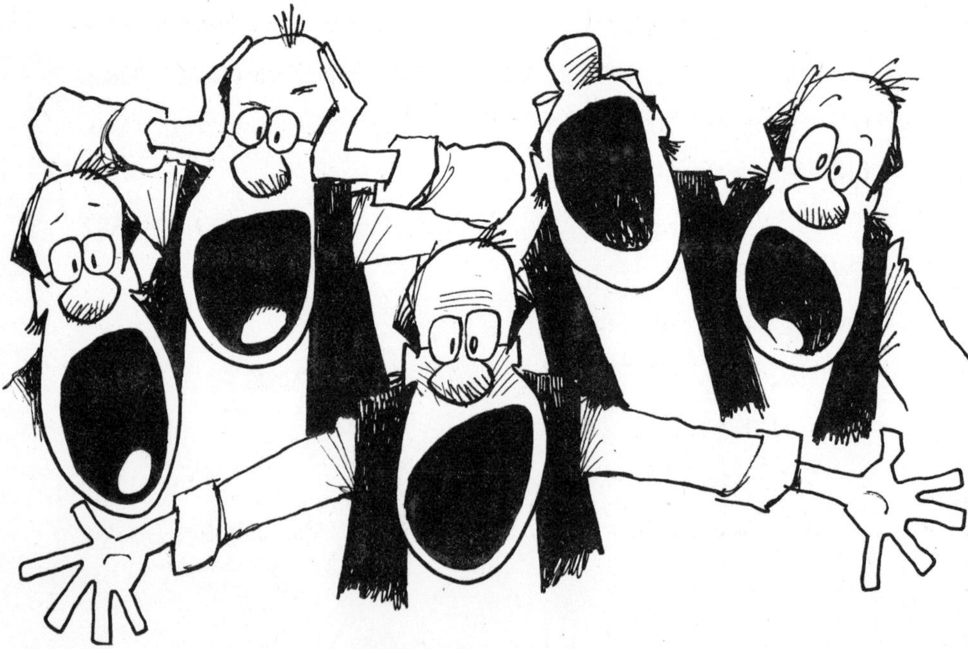

Which, I guess, is why I'm not surprised to hear hollering from upstairs as I walk in the kitchen. My mom and dad are both ridiculously nice. Even when they're yelling about something they use "please" and "thank you." Whatever is going on up there, I can tell it's not about me since the words "that kid," "knucklehead," or "grounded" aren't coming out in any familiar combinations. Something on the stove smells amazing, so I check it out.

I'm starving. A double bacon jalapeño cheeseburger just doesn't stay with me as long as it used to. There's more clomping around from upstairs, and as I drain the last milk carton, it sounds like the voices are getting closer. Placing the empty carton back in the fridge, I wonder if Mom is going to notice that she has to buy more milk before breakfast. I sure hope so.

"HONEY, ARE YOU SURE THIS IS THE SAME TUXEDO?"

"Walt, you only have one tux. Hold still."

"HERE. JUST TAKE THE PANTS, PLEASE."

"Thank you."

"YOU'RE WELCOME."

And then my dad comes rolling into the kitchen, boxer

colors flying below a tuxedo jacket that makes him look like a tube of cinnamon rolls that's just been whacked on the edge of the counter.

"I DON'T UNDERSTAND HOW A TUXEDO CAN FIT ME FOR ONE AWARDS DINNER, AND BY THE NEXT DINNER IT FEELS LIKE IT CAME FROM THE UNDERFED BOYS DEPARTMENT AT ABERCROMBIE AND FLINCH!"

My dad finally notices that I'm standing right in front of him.

"What?"

"It's Abercrombie and FITCH, dad. Not 'Flinch.'"

He stares at me for a second, then sits down at the counter and sighs. "Do you remember the Southern Ohio Orthodontic Society awards banquets your mom and I used to attend?"

"Sure," I say for the sake of avoiding further explanation.

"Well, we had no plans to attend this year's event until today, when I found out that I've been nominated for the Golden Bite Stick." Blink. Blink. Nothing registering here. "Which," he continues as he tries to wriggle out of his tux jacket, "is the big award that they give to the top orthodontist in the district." Still nothing. "It's huge," he says, "kind of a lifetime achievement award. Surely you've noticed the empty space I've left on the wall in the front hallway in case I ever receive it?"

By now I'm thinking about the flaming Dumpster of clowns with razors and I have to forcibly shake myself out of it. "Wow," I almost genuinely respond. "Very cool, Dad. Congrats."

Both his arms are behind him and he's spinning in circles, trying to get free of the tux. Pythons have an easier time shedding their skin. I grab a sleeve and tug.

"Thank you, Jeremy. The thing is, I already had plans for us to drive down to your grandma's that weekend so I could return the Pilates machine I borrowed."

"You mean the thing in your room that you hang clothes on?"

"That's the one." He grunts, finally pulling free of the second sleeve. "I obviously never got the hang of it, and she wants it back."

My mom walks in holding out what could either be a formal parachute or the bottom part of my dad's tux. "Walt, I think I might be able to let the waist out an inch or so in these pants if— Oh, hi, Jeremy."

And the next thing I know, I'm staring at the wrong end of a desperate woman's sewing scissors.

CHAPTER 3

"Jeremy . . . ?" she says again. "I'm sorry, but I have another appointment. Thanks for coming in on such short notice."

"Oh. Right! Done!" I stammer, snapping out of my fantasy and gathering up my score sheets from her desk. "This would be the time when I stand up and leave!" I'm dropping more papers than I'm managing to hold, and when she leans way over her desk to help me, I lose a few more.

Look, I don't totally understand it, but I apparently have this thing for Ms. Sparks, the sophomore guidance counselor. How else would you explain the leopard-skin leotard I just mind-dressed her in? And that's not even the most embarrassing brain candy I've ever pictured. This one time we were going over my foreign language requirements and I looked up and she was a German Hofbräu waitress with two giant mugs of beer balanced on her—um, never mind. It's not important. Ms. Sparks is this perfectly normalish adult woman who's wallpaper for every dude but me. Seriously, we have hotter lunch ladies nuking burritos in the cafeteria.

But for some reason, my hormones have decided to latch on to this guidance counselor like she's Xena: Warrior Princess in a push-up breastplate. It started when she set up monthly meetings with me after I accidentally scored a 2380 on some pre-pre-SAT exam and started getting bombed with college catalogs. Now I can't be in her office without picturing one of those book covers my mom tries not to notice when she's standing in the grocery line.

I finally manage to get the door open without making an even bigger fool of myself, but then I practically flatten Sara, Autumn, and D'ijon as I stumble out. My mental transmission grinds its gears, shifting from my Sparks fantasy to a Sara reality as I find my GF's actual face two inches from mine.

Sara looks at me with a mixture of confusion, pity, and maybe even a little nausea. Her wintergreen breath wafts around my head, and a few more of my papers fall onto the floor. She nods in Ms. Sparks's direction, smiles, and scoots by me, with Autumn and D'ijon right behind her. I glance at my phone and see that there are only a few minutes before the last bell. No sense rushing back to calculus now—not that there would ever be a reason to rush back to calculus—so I bend down to start slowly gathering up the papers I dropped. One of them has slid almost all the way under the door, and as I reach for it, I hear:

YOU'RE GETTING STARTED AWFULLY LATE, GIRLS.

BY SOPHOMORE YEAR MOST STUDENTS HAVE BEEN FUNDING THEIR NONPROFIT FOUNDATIONS THROUGH VARIOUS FUND-RAISING ACTIVITIES AND ARE DEALING WITH EXCESS CONTRIBUTIONS VIA NONTAXABLE CARRYOVERS.

BLINK!

BLINK! BLINK!

YOUR ELEMENTARY SCHOOL GUIDANCE COUNSELORS SHOULD HAVE HELPED YOU ESTABLISH YOUR 501(c)(3)s YEARS AGO.

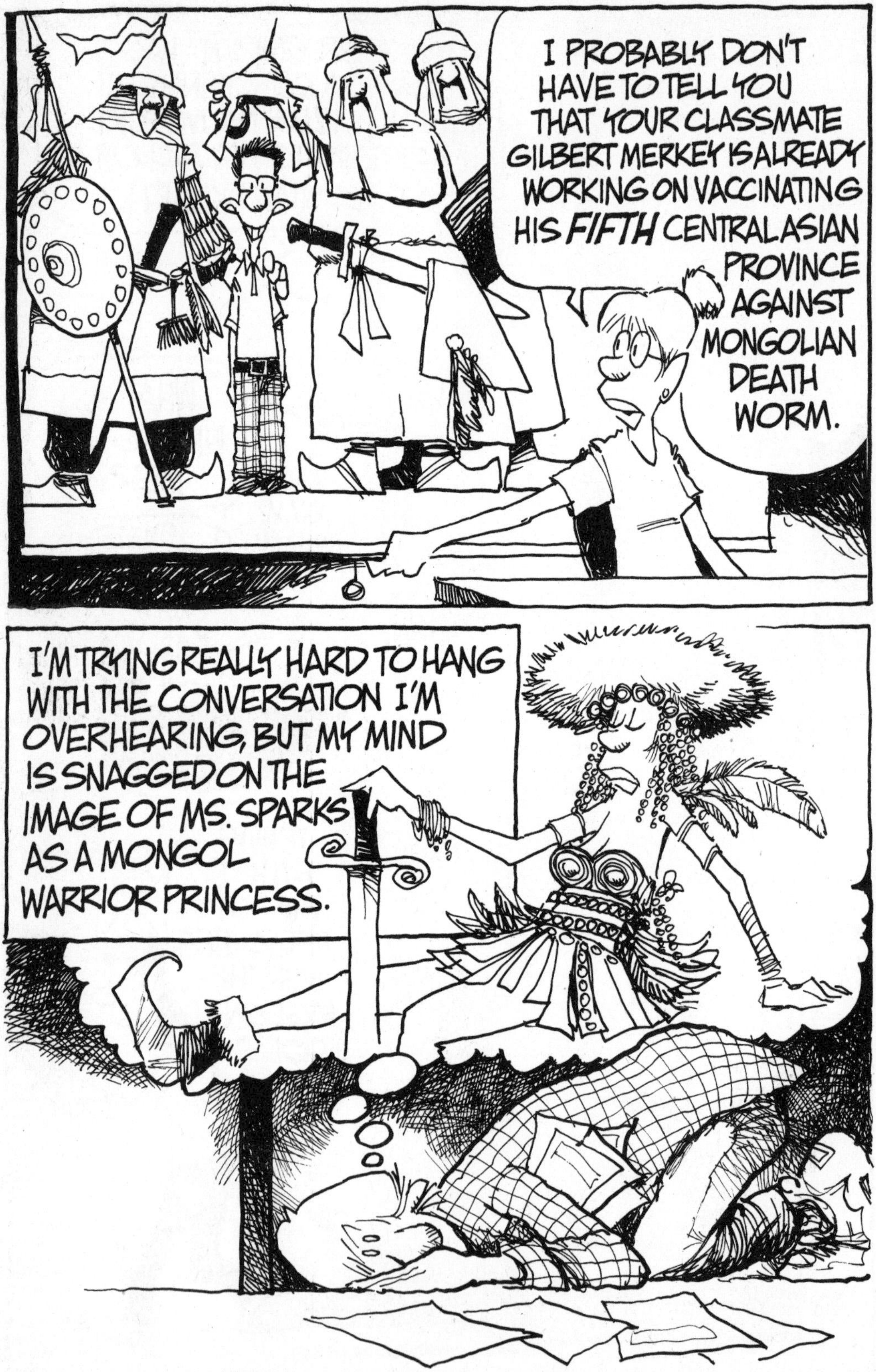
I PROBABLY DON'T HAVE TO TELL YOU THAT YOUR CLASSMATE GILBERT MERKEY IS ALREADY WORKING ON VACCINATING HIS *FIFTH* CENTRAL ASIAN PROVINCE AGAINST MONGOLIAN DEATH WORM.
I'M TRYING REALLY HARD TO HANG WITH THE CONVERSATION I'M OVERHEARING, BUT MY MIND IS SNAGGED ON THE IMAGE OF MS. SPARKS AS A MONGOL WARRIOR PRINCESS.

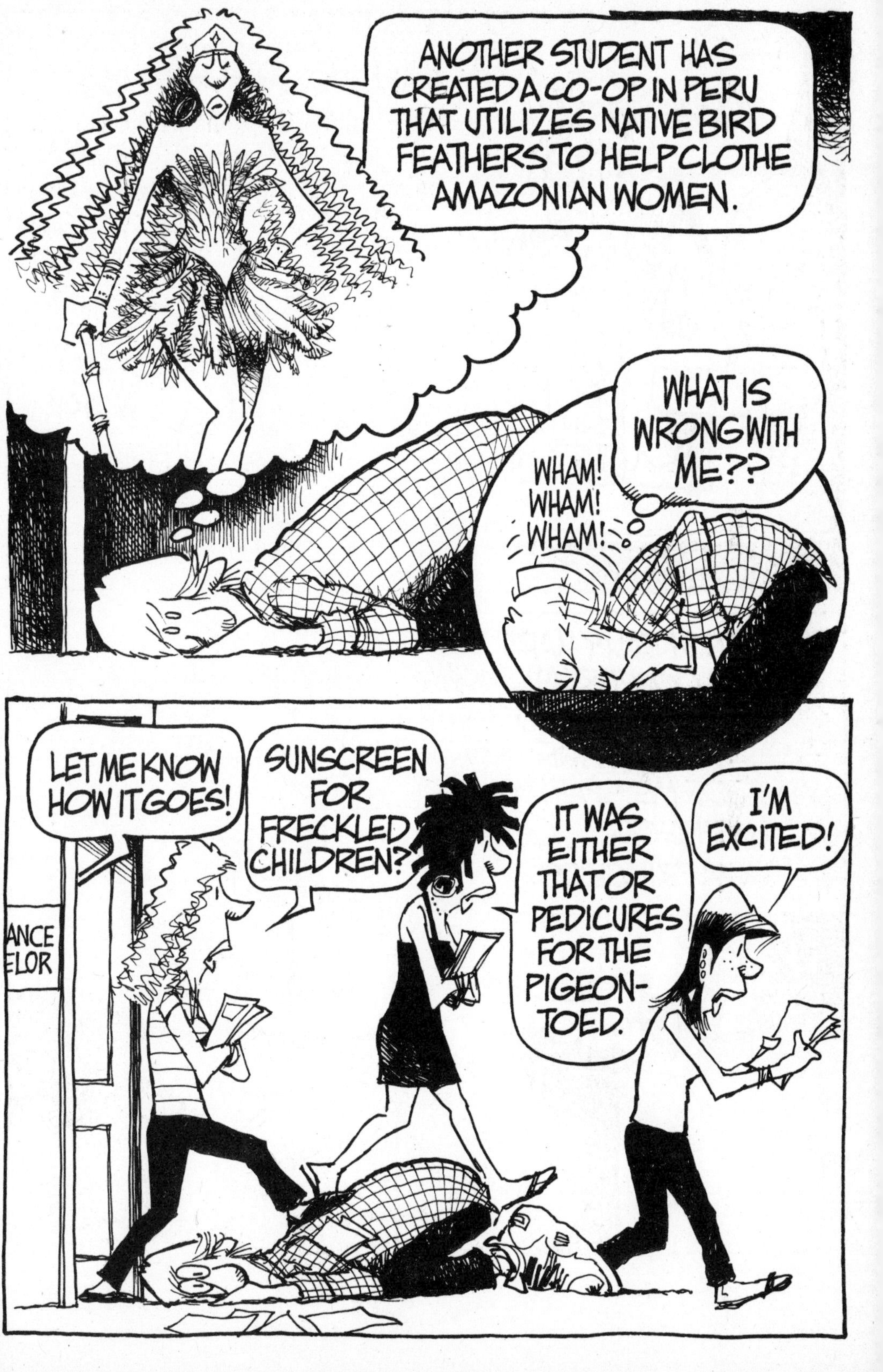
ANOTHER STUDENT HAS CREATED A CO-OP IN PERU THAT UTILIZES NATIVE BIRD FEATHERS TO HELP CLOTHE AMAZONIAN WOMEN.
WHAT IS WRONG WITH ME??
WHAM! WHAM! WHAM!
LET ME KNOW HOW IT GOES!
ANCE
ELOR
SUNSCREEN FOR FRECKLED CHILDREN?
IT WAS EITHER THAT OR PEDICURES FOR THE PIGEON-TOED.
I'M EXCITED!

Okay, so it looks like the girls have their public-service deal lined up. Sunscreen for Freckled Children doesn't sound as sexy as, say, Death Worm Vaccinations, but, hey, a project is a project. If it'll help get us into college, that's all that counts. I pick my stuff up and brush some of the footprints off my back and head toward the van.

This has been such a weird day, but as I pull up to my house I can see that there's still more to come. I have been driving up our driveway every day since I qualified for my learner's permit. Besides that one time when I modestly clipped the rear fender of my mom's car and it had to be towed out of the neighbors' pool, I have been nearly accident-free. Of course, that never stops her from offering me a little helpful assistance.

I can tell by the way my mom is jumping up and down and tearing at her hair that I must be getting close to her car's bumper, so I stop. Another perfect parking job. I take my foot off the clutch and the van lurches forward two inches and I feel a little bump. I believe that's why they call them bumpers, so yeah. Whoops. My mom sighs as she trudges back into the house, and I grab my backpack and beat her to the kitchen. I need a snack.

It's a well-known fact that by the time school is out my lunch has worn off and I'm on the hunt for nutrition. Yet somehow this always surprises and annoys my mom, causing tons of moaning and groaning about grocery bills, ruined meals, and teeth marks on the fridge door. I don't think I'm that extreme about food, but after about twenty minutes of being lectured on how I'm that extreme about food, I decide that it's time to derail her train of thought.

"So about that orthodontist award thing and my plans for that weekend," I wedge in while she's taking a breath.

"Ohmygawd. Your father is obsessing about his tuxedo. I finally had to tell him that we should just go rent one and—"

"Yeah," I interrupt again. "Switching back to the Jeremy Channel for a moment, can I ask how mandatory this Pilates machine delivery thing is? Because it sounds like a real drag."

Okay, that didn't go so well. Apparently mandatory still means mandatory. Good to know.

"Your dad promised Grandma that she'd get her exercise machine back later this month," she growls. "And there's no way we can do it since we'll be in Chillicothe at the awards dinner."

I should be hatching a howling protest of a response at this point, but my mind is hung up as it flashes to an image of my grandma exercising on the Pilates contraption.

Ohmygawd. I think I just threw up in my mouth. I stick my head under the faucet and turn it on. I gulp down about a gallon of cold water, drowning out any image fragments of an old lady in a leotard and restoring my visual cortex's photo bank to the usual array of YouTube pranks, girl parts, and vintage guitars. My mom is just standing there staring at me. The line in the sand has been drawn, and there's no getting out of this, so I do the only logical thing: I whine.

Hold on, something just vibrated in my brain.

Whoa, whoa, whoa. Must exercise great caution here.

This is it! The Golden Ticket has been sitting right in front of me and I didn't even see it. It's the perfect opportunity for a road trip! Nobody said that a hundred-mile trip to my grandma's house had to be only a hundred miles, right? With my parents tied up at the Golden Bite Me Award (or whatever it's called), the guys and I can totally hit about three states and really get a preview of the Big Trip we've been planning for.

Come on, Jeremy. Control your breathing. Look put out. I sigh a deep sigh and pitch forward, burying my face in my arms.

"Fine. I'll do it."

I take the stairs up to my room three at a time while group texting Hector and Pierce, and meet my dad in the hallway. He has a yellow measuring tape cinched tight around his waist and

is trying to read it
upside down while
muttering some-
thing about salad
for breakfast.

"I talked to Mom.
You don't have to worry about
Grandma's Pilates machine. I'll
get it to her, no problem."

"Yeah. That's a good idea,
Jeremy. I'll just go rent a tux instead
of worrying about this one. Plus, I have to
write an acceptance speech. Not that I think
I'm going to win the Golden Bite Stick or anything.
Just in case, you know? Better to always be prepared in life,
right?"

"Yeah," I un-agree. "Speaking of driving, since I don't ask
you for gas money now that the van runs on veggie oil, do you
think I could get some french fry funds instead?"

"Mmm . . . french fries," he says. Then he looks down at
the measuring tape that's pinned under his belly fat and sighs.
"I probably won't be pounding down too many of them for a
while. At least not 'til the award weekend is over." Reaching for
his back pocket, which isn't there since he's still not wearing
any pants, he says, "Hang on . . . let me grab my wallet." And
while he lumbers down the hall, I finish the text to Hector and
Pierce.

"Dudes," it reads. "The Cross-country Canola Crusade is happening! Make sure you're free on the 24th. Details at practice in 1 hr." I push Send and slip into my room. Two seconds later there's a knock on my doorframe. I stick my head out and find Ulysses S. Grant staring me in the face.

"Here's fifty bucks," my dad says.

CHAPTER 4

"There it is!" Pierce is standing on his tiptoes, the way he does when he's totally amped about something. "Right there! Did you hear the bass?" Hector, Tim, and I are leaning on my dad's workbench, listening to Pierce's turntable in my garage. We're supposed to be practicing, but Hector started pushing Pierce's buttons about analog versus digital recording, and that's like asking Mr. Stumpwaller, the government teacher, if conservatives aren't basically the same as liberals. It's a guaranteed rant.

"So you're one of those guys who believes that CDs and MP3s don't sound as good as vinyl records," presses Hector.

"It's not something I believe . . . it's a stone-cold fact! Real musicians understand this."

I really like listening to Pierce and Hector go at it. There's something almost musical about Pierce's high-key voice yammering the melody of his argument against the deeper timbre (cool word, right? Thanks, Wikipedia!) of Hector's questions and laughter.

"Plus, vinyl is just much cooler. Listening to music should be an experience for all the senses," says Pierce. Now he's squatting on the workbench next to his turntable and practically making out with the album jacket. "There's nothing like sliding a record out of its sleeve, placing it on the turntable, dropping the needle in the groove, and then sitting back and listening to music the way it was intended to be heard . . ."

I have to admit that the record sounds pretty good. When Pierce turns the bass up, the old paint cans above our heads skitter toward the edge of the shelf, and I can feel the vibration down into my lower back. You know that you're hearing a good song when it vibrates your skeleton. Pierce's eyes roll up in their sockets as the deep thrum oozes out of the speaker cabinet. He gets a big grin on his face and says, "That, dudes, is what is known as a fat, fuzzy bottom."

"So is that," I say. "But around here, we just call him Dad." Pierce starts laughing that horselaugh of his, Tim snorts, and Hector fist-bumps me. I stick my head out the side door to make sure that my dad is going into the house, then slip back to the workbench and twist the volume knob way down. "So everybody is good to go on the twenty-fourth?"

"Count me out," says Tim.

Damn! That's right! He hasn't been able to ride in the van

since we had the new engine put in, due to a rare french fry allergy. Seriously, his doctor told him that the air inside a veggie oil–powered van would be as toxic to him as the atmosphere on Venus.

I guess Tim is one of those people who are just sensitive to environmental pollutants.

Or, maybe not.

"Plus, I'm at level nine in Shoot and Blow Stuff Up II, so, yeah. No. When I'm not gagging roaches, I'll be on the couch wreaking havoc with my Xbox."

Respectful nods all around. Level nine is pretty awesome, especially on SABSU II.

Okay, so Tim can't go. That's one down.

Hector messes with the tuners on his guitar and says,

I look at Pierce, and he nods. Sure.

We're set. All I have to do is maintain the whiny, victimized attitude with my parents about having to drive my grandma's Pilates machine to her house. No problem. Whiny and victimized are my default settings.

"Great," I say, switching to my mastermind mode. "We'll eventually need to make a Costco run for provisions and twenty gallons of canola oil. That'll be insurance to get us home, in case we can't scrounge enough fries to squeeze into the van's tank." I look down and notice a puddle of saliva forming around my shoes.

I should know better than to mention Costco with Hector in the room. The dude's hungry most of the time, but once the thought of those barrel-size containers of cashews and beef jerky gets his salivary glands working, the only thing to do is tie a beach towel around his neck and hit the warehouse. I start looking around for a mop before Hector's digestive juices electrocute us all, when . . .

All of our band practices are closed sessions, so the only people who know we're here are my parents and the neighbors, who always whine about the noise. I guess we've reached the point where the complaints start before we even play a chord, which I take as a huge compliment. Looking back at the guys, I shrug and they shrug back. Then I take a deep breath and open the door.

I don't know about you, but when confronted by a group of excited girls in cutoff jeans, I step back and listen. Resistance is futile. D'ijon flaps her hands a few times and stifles a squeal.

"Okay, okay! You know the sucky public-service project we got?"

"Sunscreen for Freckled Children," explains Autumn.

Then Sara stamps her foot and yells, "I wish you guys would stop calling it sucky! It's a good cause!"

"All right, all right. I'm sorry again," groans D'ijon. And then she starts jumping up and down, re-excited. "Anyway, we had this great idea that Goat Cheese Pizza could be the spokesband for the cause!"

Deafening silence.

CHIRP
CHIRP
CHIRP

"You know . . . to really get attention for the fund-raiser we're putting together," chimes Sara. "What do you think?"

The guys and I look at each other. Then Hector clears his throat and says, "I think that we should go pick up those cashews now."

It's hard to argue with that kind of logic, and I immediately start to see the merits of the idea, thanks to the way Sara is scratching my back. Tim rolls his eyes and turns to leave when I see Sara reach over and start to scratch his back, too. Like that's going to work.

Okay, it's working.

"And it would be so cool," Sara says as her fingers trace the outline of the knobby trail of my backbone, "if you could write and record a song for the Freckled Children that we could sell."

"Like burning some CDs," I say.

"Or posting an MP3 and asking for donations," suggests Hector.

Pierce runs over to his drum kit yelling, "No! No! Wait! I got it!"

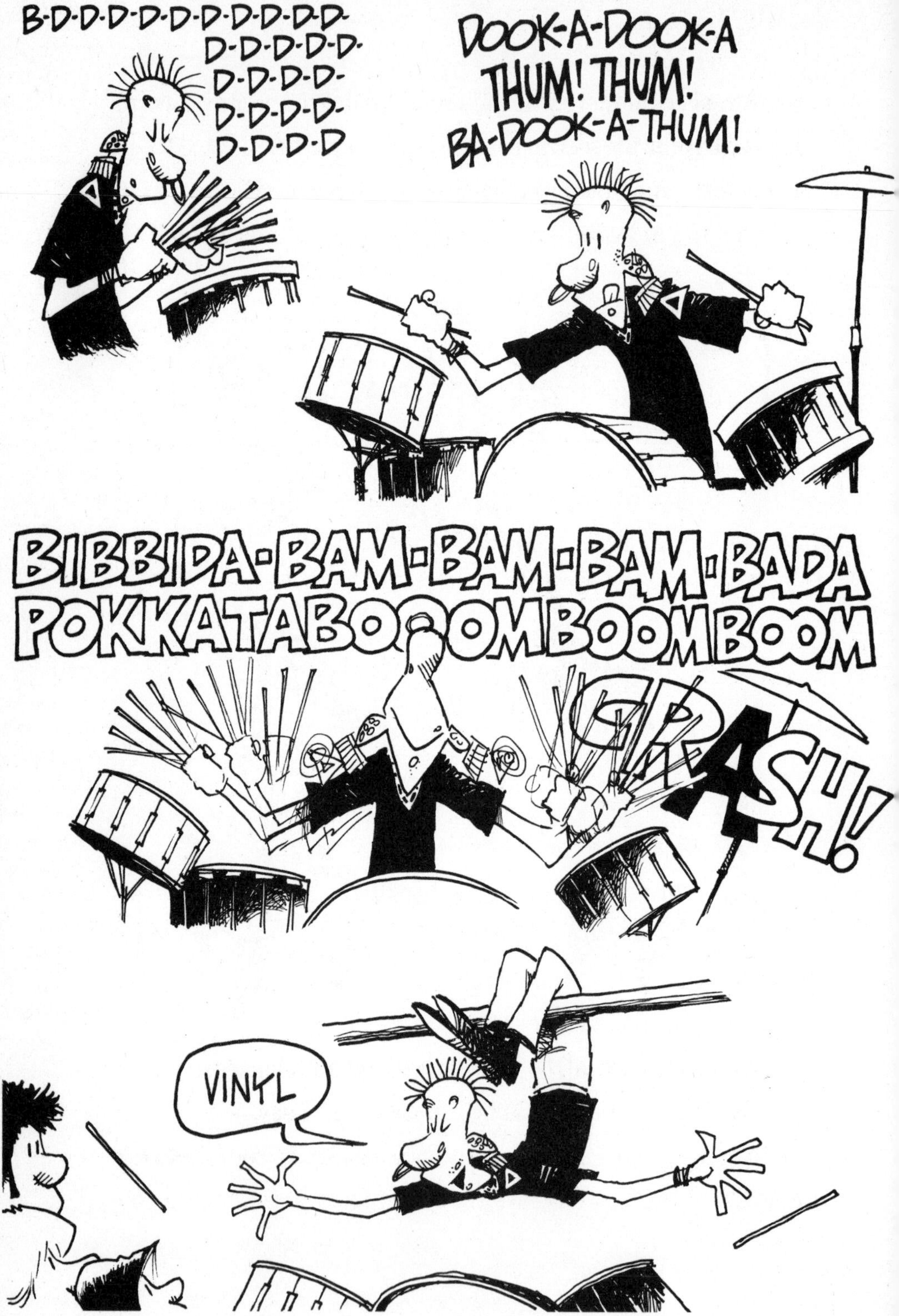
B-D-D-D-D-D-D-D-D-D-D-D-D-D-D-D-D-D-D-D-D-D-D-D-D-D-D-D-D-D-D-D-D-D-D-D
DOOK-A-DOOK-A
THUM! THUM!
BA-DOOK-A-THUM!
BIBBIDA-BAM-BAM-BAM-BADA
POKKATABOOOMBOOMBOOM
CRASH!
VINYL

"Vinyl," I repeat.

"A real record," confirms Pierce. "We write a song, record it, and have it pressed. We could even have the Goat Cheese Pizza logo embedded in it! What could be cooler?"

That has to be the stupidest thing I've ever heard.

But now it's actually starting to sound better to me.

"Cutting a record would be kind of cool," I say.

"Not just cool," says Pierce. "Epic. Epically cool. Epicool. And I know exactly how we can do it." Then he lowers himself onto the ground and herds Sara, Autumn, and D'ijon out of the garage. "Come with me, girls."

Hector and Tim look at me. There's a long, awkward silence as we try to figure out what we just agreed to do, and then I say the only thing that comes to mind.

CHAPTER 5

In the three weeks and two days since I agreed to drive the Pilates machine back to my grandma's place, our plans and supplies for the road trip have expanded like a marshmallow Peep in a microwave. But the day is finally here and it feels awesome. The girls don't know it yet, but we've decided to write and record the Freckled Children track on the road . . . as if this trip wasn't cool enough already!

Hector loads the last batch of snacks we've just picked up from Costco into the van while I arrange them. And by "arrange," I mean jamming as much stuff as I can under the stupid Pilates machine, which takes up most of the floor space back here. He heaves a plastic barrel full of Red Vines up and shoves it toward me. For empty calories, they weigh a ton. I kick it into place against the dried meats and hot sauces just in time. Nice. That and a couple of bungees should keep it from overbalancing and smashing anything on the chips pallet, which is strategically placed within easy reaching distance of the driver's seat. In fact, the whole van is a junk food paradise. I predict that my mom will be changing the PIN on her ATM card after this.

"Once we get the rest of the stuff in here, it'll lock everything in place snackwise," I say, with no small amount of pride. I learned to pack a vehicle from watching my dad get us ready for family vacations. Nobody can cram more unnecessary junk into a vehicle than my dad.

I'm just getting the cocktail weenies wedged between the Skittles and the Roquefort-stuffed olives when I see Pierce and Hector stick their heads in the door.

"What did I tell you?" says Hector to Pierce. "This should get us there and back, no matter where we're going."

"Impressive," says Pierce.

"Yeah, speaking of that," I say, breaking the seal on the Twizzlers. "Where *are* we going?"

Pierce sighs, reaches behind me for a chunk of beef jerky, and settles in. "Sheboygan," he announces through the peppery meat chaw.

"You shouldn't talk with your mouth full of dried beef, because it sounded like you just said Sheboygan," says Hector.

"I did," Pierce confirms, wiping the grease off his mouth with one hand and pulling his phone out of his pocket with the other. "Sheboygan via Kickstarter. It's a beautiful plan. I have it all worked out . . . observe:"

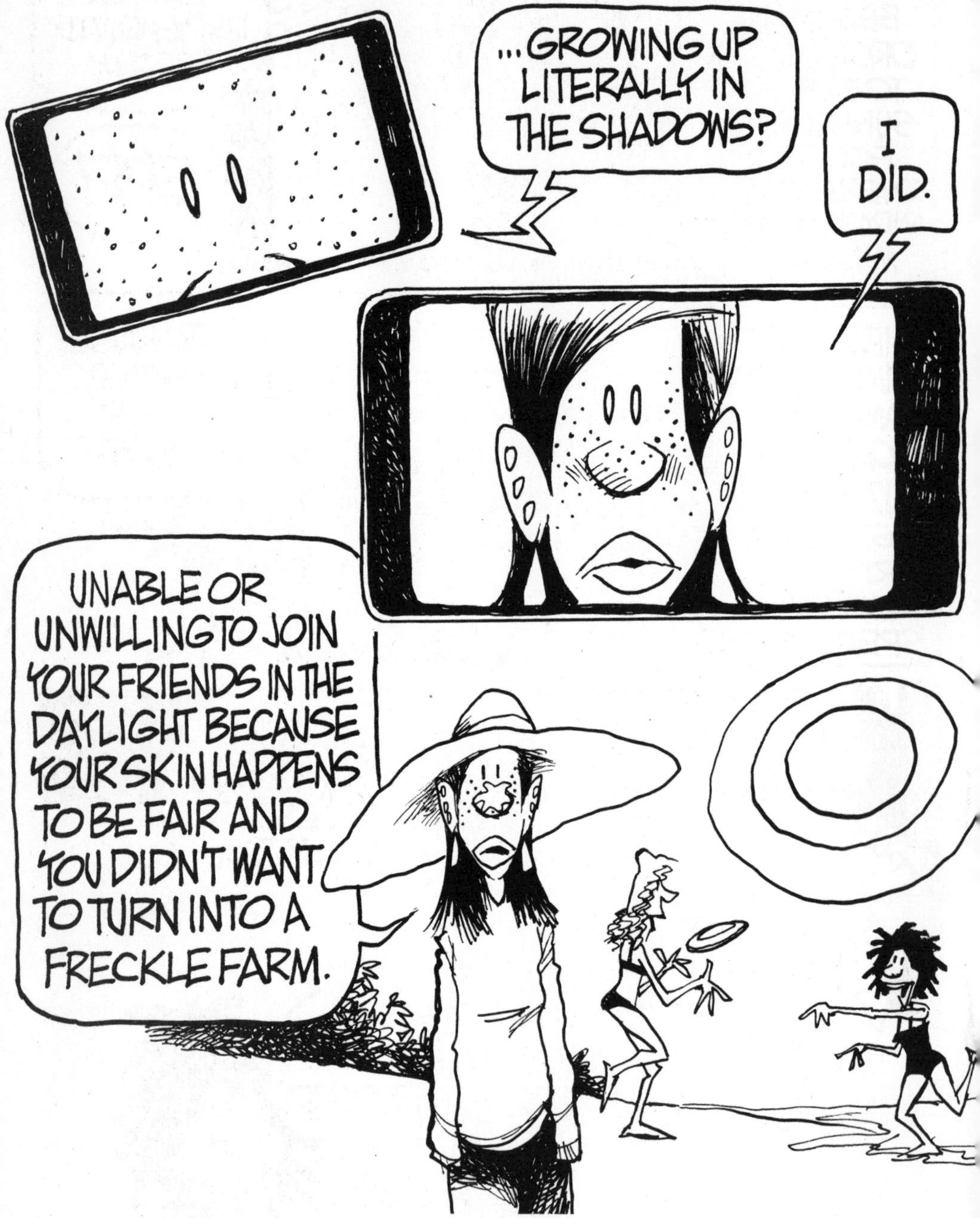
...GROWING UP LITERALLY IN THE SHADOWS?
I DID.
UNABLE OR UNWILLING TO JOIN YOUR FRIENDS IN THE DAYLIGHT BECAUSE YOUR SKIN HAPPENS TO BE FAIR AND YOU DIDN'T WANT TO TURN INTO A FRECKLE FARM.

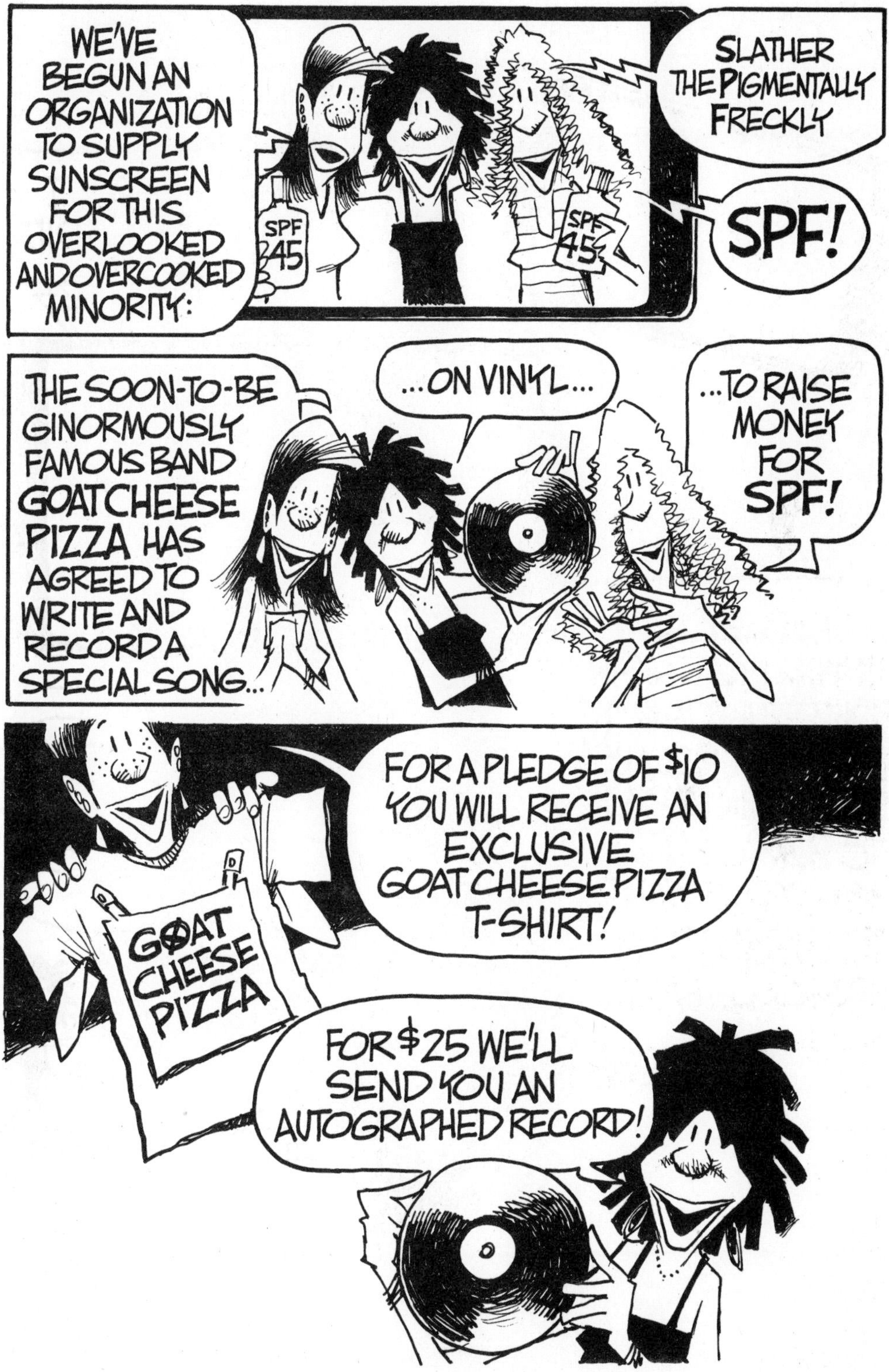
WE'VE BEGUN AN ORGANIZATION TO SUPPLY SUNSCREEN FOR THIS OVERLOOKED AND OVERCOOKED MINORITY:
SPF 45
SPF 45
SLATHER THE PIGMENTALLY FRECKLY
SPF!
THE SOON-TO-BE GINORMOUSLY FAMOUS BAND GOAT CHEESE PIZZA HAS AGREED TO WRITE AND RECORD A SPECIAL SONG...
...ON VINYL...
...TO RAISE MONEY FOR SPF!
FOR A PLEDGE OF $10 YOU WILL RECEIVE AN EXCLUSIVE GOAT CHEESE PIZZA T-SHIRT!
GOAT CHEESE PIZZA
FOR $25 WE'LL SEND YOU AN AUTOGRAPHED RECORD!

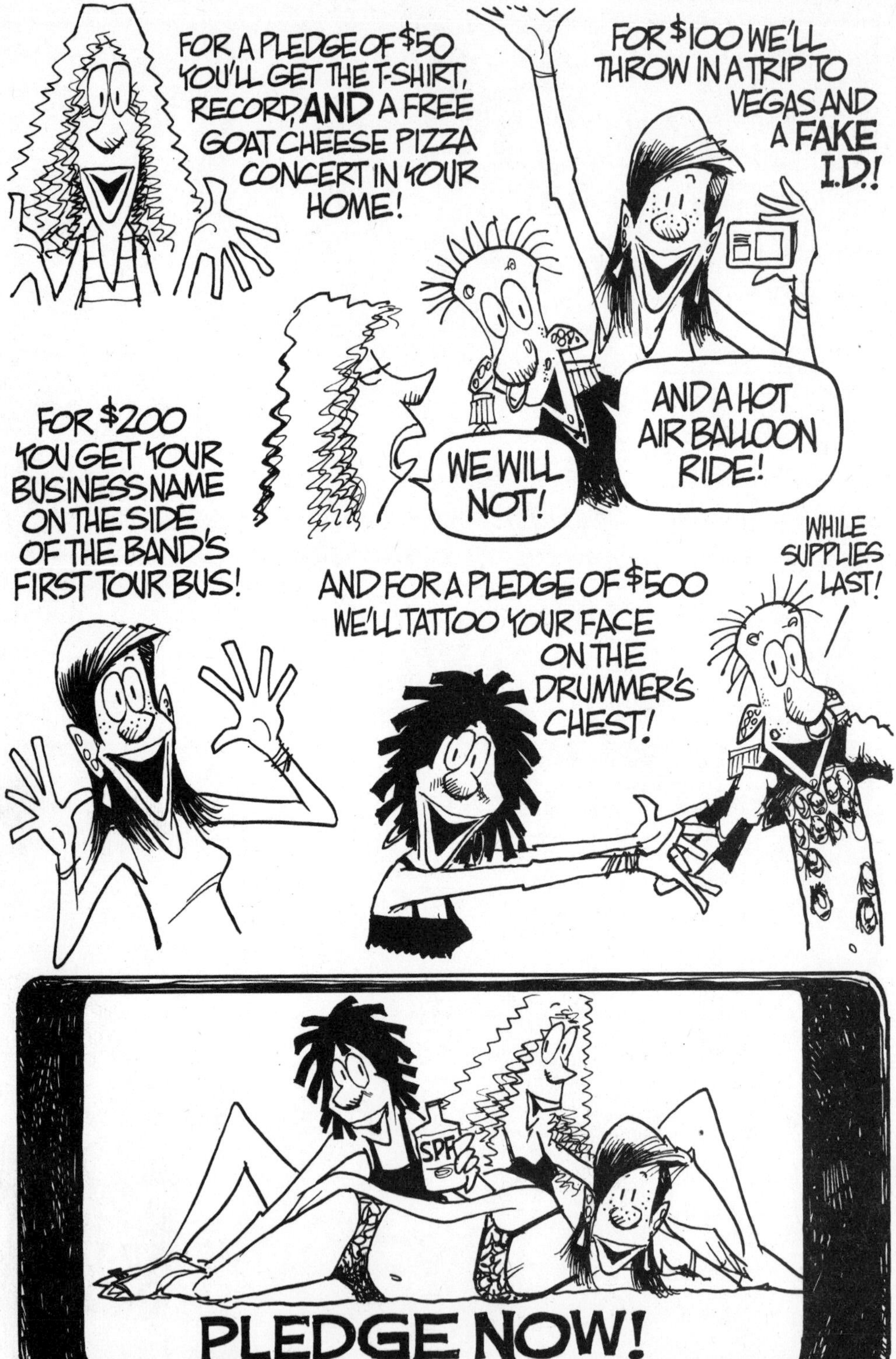
FOR A PLEDGE OF $50 YOU'LL GET THE T-SHIRT, RECORD, AND A FREE GOAT CHEESE PIZZA CONCERT IN YOUR HOME!
FOR $100 WE'LL THROW IN A TRIP TO VEGAS AND A FAKE I.D.!
AND A HOT AIR BALLOON RIDE!
WE WILL NOT!
FOR $200 YOU GET YOUR BUSINESS NAME ON THE SIDE OF THE BAND'S FIRST TOUR BUS!
AND FOR A PLEDGE OF $500 WE'LL TATTOO YOUR FACE ON THE DRUMMER'S CHEST!
WHILE SUPPLIES LAST!
SPF
PLEDGE NOW!

"Whoa," says Hector.

"Agreed," I say. "Where do I send the money?"

Pierce clicks out of the Kickstarter page and grins. "With a little luck, this video is going to pay for veggie oil and any expenses we'll need to make this record. Anything left over gets donated to the cause."

"No offense, but Sheboygan seems kind of random," I say, tearing open a package of Funyuns.

Actually, that is kind of cool.

"But half price is still six hundred bucks, dude," say Hector as he taps on his maps app. "Plus, Sheboygan is four hundred forty-one miles away. That's about three hundred and fifty bucks' worth of french fry grease alone. Is the Kickstarter going to make that much money?"

"I dunno. Maybe. Who cares?" Pierce shrugs. "We can use

my emergency credit card for expenses."

I have two thoughts here: One, our drummer has actually come up with a workable plan, and two, he has a credit card???

Pierce scrolls through the website, then stops. "The Kickstarter has been live for twenty-seven minutes, and so far we've raised . . ."

ONE HUNDRED FORTY-THREE THOUSAND EIGHT HUNDRED FIFTY DOLLARS

"That's good, right?" he asks.

"Yeah. That's, um, good," Hector says, staring at me.

I look over Pierce's shoulder and read something else.

"Plus some guy who owns a chicken wing joint in

Bloomington says he'll give us eighty gallons of used veggie oil for fuel."

My dad has always told me that making money is a hard, slow process, and he was right. That took part of an afternoon.

"So, are we ready?" Pierce has clicked out of the Kickstarter site and is shoving a crate of some kind behind the Cheetos. I look at Hector and he shrugs.

"Let's do this," he says, and I start the engine, which drenches us in the sweet aroma of fast-food grease.

"Smells like independence," I say, rolling the window down anyway. Suddenly I've become aware of the overwhelming smell of hand lotion and spearmint gum wafting in my direction. "Bye, Mom," I say without even looking up. And slip the van into reverse.

"And your Triple A card? Do you want me to make a list of emergency phone numbers you can call, just in case?" My mom is clinging to my window frame like it's the last slow dance at a junior high prom.

"Yes, Mom. No, Mom. Don't worry, Mom. We'll be fine." I mentally calculate the parental blowback I'd get if I just started rolling up my window, but it's pretty warm out, so I don't.

"Did you bring enough clothes? It might rain." Typical Mom, always assuming that we're still a bunch of immature middle schoolers instead of responsible young adults. I consider telling her how we each thought ahead and packed a pair of clean boxers. Pierce even brought a toothbrush that we can share if necessary, but she would probably find something to criticize about that, too. Guys travel light. Given the choice between three suitcases or fourteen liters of Mountain Dew, the Mountain Dew wins.

"What about floss?"

"Mom . . ."

"You know how your father feels about dental hygiene."

"I know. He's an orthodontist. He can't help it."

"Do you have a map to Grandma's condo?" I feel an invisible leash tightening around my neck, but I keep my cool and politely answer between pleasantly gritted teeth.

"I have her address in my contacts and a smart phone. I could find her in a bunker, Mom."

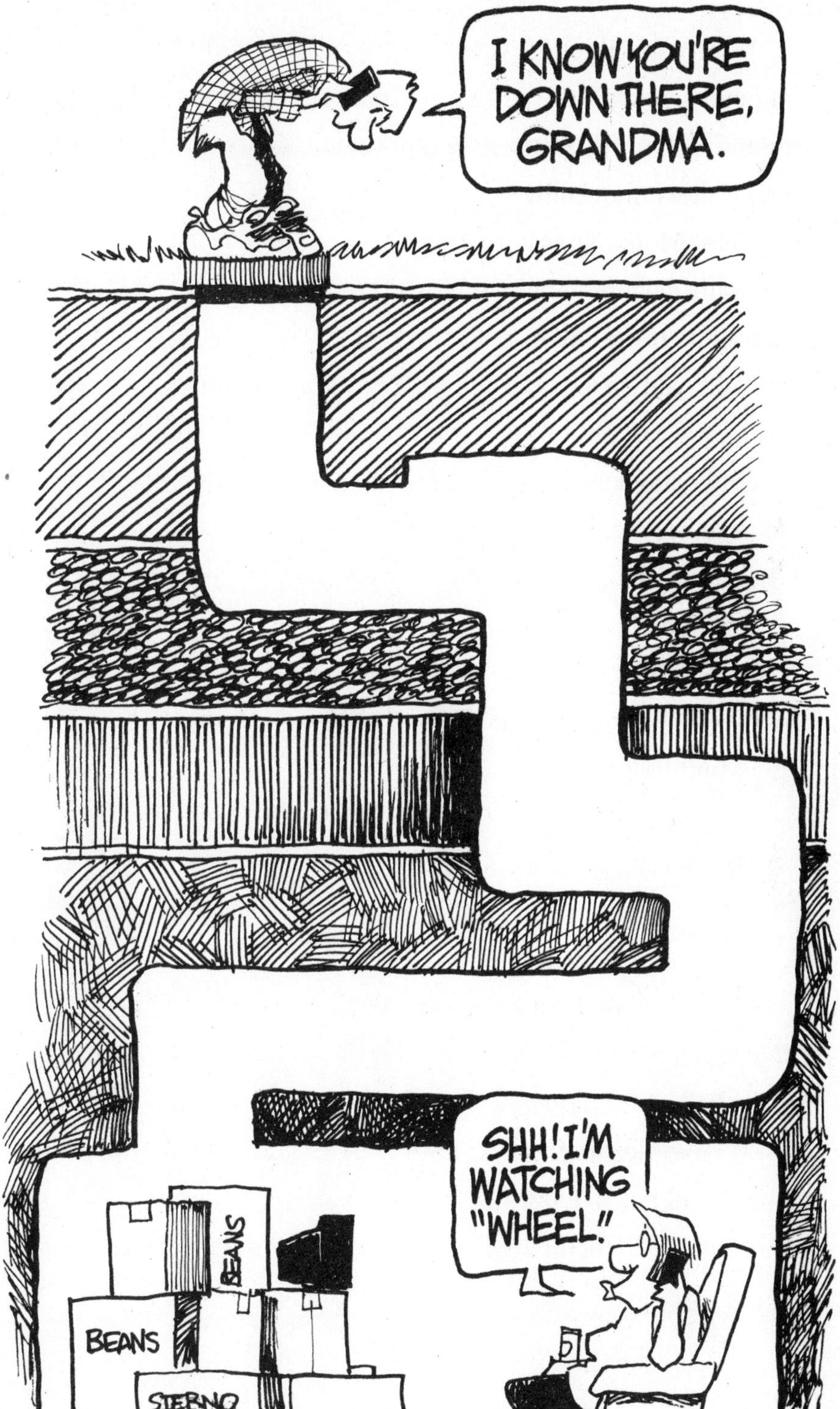
I KNOW YOU'RE DOWN THERE, GRANDMA.
SHH! I'M WATCHING "WHEEL."
BEANS
BEANS
STERNO

"How long do you think the trip will take?" I feel Hector shift in his seat and Pierce's eyebrow rings jingle softly as his eyes roll upward. We're sitting in the middle of the street now, and it feels like the whole neighborhood is watching my mom change my diaper or something.

"At this rate, about thirty-six hours. Mom, I'm fine! Now just let us go, okay?"

"Well, be sure to call and tell Grandma when to expect you, but—"

And then I hit the gas—well, veggie oil—and we are rolling.

Freedom! Hector reaches over and spins the volume knob on the stereo, I hang my elbow out the window, and life is good again. Sort of. What is it about not telling your parents the whole truth that seems almost dishonest?

"If it makes you feel any better," Hector says, "my mom made me promise, like, ten times that I would stay out of trouble and use my head. This is the first time I've gone anywhere by myself! I don't even know what my misbehavior options are!"

It's obvious that this trip is a totally cool thing to be doing, but we need some witnesses if we're going to get the full benefit. What good is being cool if nobody is there to see it and tell other people about it? So I hang a left and start cruising down some streets where we're likely to be seen by somebody we know. A band survives on reputation and legend, and this is the time to start building ours. No such luck.

We must have driven through half a dozen neighborhoods and haven't seen a single— Wait! Around the corner and about halfway down the block I see Chelsea-from-My-Econ-Class sitting on a towel in the grass. I hang a left and yell at Hector and Pierce that I spotted somebody, which, as I'm doing it, already seems like a mistake.

The words are barely out of my mouth before Hector is practically in my lap and Pierce is trying to scramble over the backseat. He plants a foot on the bottom case of Strawberry Quik, and I hear it start to slide across the floor. "No! No! No! That's too much weight on this side! You guys back off!" In my rearview mirror I can see the whole stack of drinks tilt left and then start to fall. I slam on the brakes, but it's too late. There's a small, surrendering groan from the suspension, and the last thing I see is a slow-motion sideways view of Chelsea-from-My-Econ-Class getting it all on video.

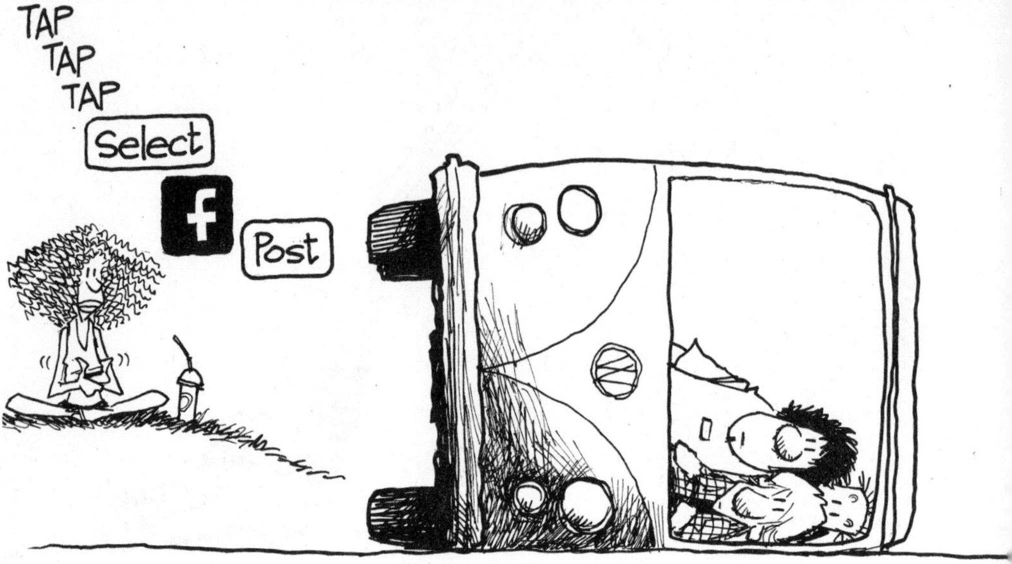
TAP
TAP
TAP
Select
Post

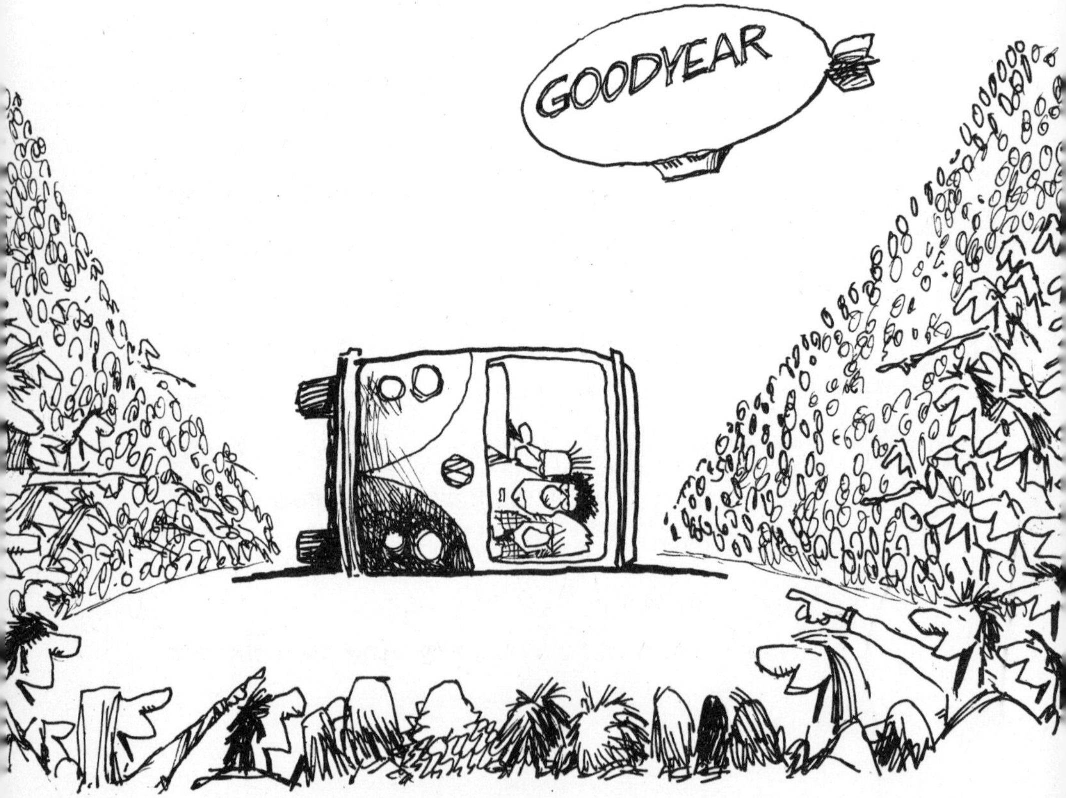
GOODYEAR

Well, that could have turned out better.

"Sara's house is, like, a block from here," I say as I start the engine. "Let's just swing past and say good-bye."

"Mistake," mumbles Pierce from the back, where he's restacking the tortilla tower that's now more of a plateau. The snack food avalanche smashed most of our chips, so we'll be scooping bean dip and salsa by hand. It's a major bummer, but at least the guy in the back will have room to straighten his legs now. Hector starts noodling with a melody (in a minor key) on his guitar, and I pull off the curb as carefully as possible in order to avoid any further YouTube exposure of our group lameness. Man, even the van seems bummed. When I push on the accelerator, there's less power than usual. In fact, a LOT less power. Pierce cocks his head and listens.

"Sounds like a clog in the fuel line."

"Yeah," I agree without knowing why. And then the van

limps the last few yards to Sara's house like a tree sloth with a bad case of plantar fasciitis. Question: Could this trip get any suckier?

Answer: What do you think?

Sara pokes me in the chest and says, "You know, we have been busting our butts making posters and planning this thing for weeks."

"That's right," agrees D'ijon. "How's that song coming? Huh? We need that record in three days. Almost finished?"

"Almost *started*," answers Pierce from deep inside the engine compartment.

"You know, we could just do this thing without you. In fact, it might be better if we did," snaps Autumn in Pierce's direction. Those two don't really get along too well. She's wound pretty tight, and, as my mom would say, Pierce's thread is barely on the spool.

"Good suggestion, Autumn," hollers Pierce.

"Thank you. Oh! And guess what? We just found out that we have to use the school parking lot for the fund-raiser, so there's even more space to fill with people!"

This community service project is starting to lose its appeal. All the guys and I wanted to do was to have a good time recording a song while the girls did most of the work. Now it feels like they're in charge.

"It'll be okay, don't worry," says Pierce as he crawls out of the engine compartment. "And you might want to move away from that tailpipe."

Autumn makes an exasperated noise and stomps over to Hector and glares at him. Pierce motions at me to start the engine, and I move from the interpersonal tension into the driver's seat. When I turn the key, there's a choking sound, then a cough, then nothing except snickers from the girls.

"Hang on," says Pierce as he bangs on something engine-ish. Then, "Okay. Try it again!"

Whatever it is that shoots out of the tailpipe skids across the yard and comes to a stop at Hector's feet. D'ijon says, "What is that?"

Hector picks it up, turns it over a couple of times, and takes a bite. "Filet-O-Fish," he announces.

"Guys, how many times do I have to remind you to strain the grease before you put it in the tank?" Pierce is slamming his tools back in the bag, the girls are gagging, and the engine sounds as happy as my dad after a bran muffin and coffee.

"Gotta jump," I holler, and the guys pile in. We wave to the girls as they stand there in our triglyceride exhaust cloud, stomping their feet and yelling responsibility-related threats, but we can't hear them through the joy.

Two blocks later, all our cell phones start vibrating. Hector picks his up and says, "More Freckled Children fund-raiser tasks." We all look at each other, and then:

But then:

Okay, we may not be totally free, but we're finally on the road with nothing in front of us now but weekend and asphalt.

CHAPTER 6

AHHHHHHHHHHHHHH!

We may be driving a veggie oil–powered van, but we still need gas stations. This one is about a mile outside Bloomington, Indiana, so we have almost officially made it to the first stop on the tour. I'm calling it that because "tour" sounds better than "random trip to Sheboygan." The guy behind the counter hollers something about the restrooms being for customers only, so Pierce puts a quarter in the gumball machine on the way out the door.

I pull onto the highway and glance over at Hector.

"Navigator . . . ?"

"Take a left at the next light, go seven-eighths of a mile, then turn right," he says. "In eight hundred and three feet you will hit a small, oblong pothole, and the destination will be on your right."

And there it is, exactly where he said it would be.

"What app are you using?" I ask Hector. "Because it's dead-on accurate, dude."

"No app," he says, leaning forward and resting his elbows

on his knees. He stares out the window and swipes a hand over the puddle of drool that's forming at the corner of his mouth.

The gravel in the parking lot crunches under our tires like deep-fried Bubble Wrap as I pull up to the restaurant, conveniently situated between a used textbook store and a hookah parlor. You gotta love college towns.

We can hear some really cheesy eighties rock 'n' roll coming from inside, and we can already tell that this is going to be our kind of place. I ease into a parking space right below the rusting neon sign, which says it all.

There's enough grease in the air that we could probably fill up our fuel tank by just sitting here with the gas cap off, but Chunky promised us eighty gallons of used veggie oil, and we're going to collect. It's a long way to Sheboygan. Hector spots a menu taped to the window by the front door and grunts. Pierce looks over his shoulder and gives a low whistle.

"*Rolling Stone* calls Chunky's 'the hottest hot wings this side of the third ring of hell,'" he says. "'At one million three hundred seventy thousand Scoville units, they're hotter than the Trinidad Moruga Scorpion pepper and only slightly milder than Mace.'"

"They used to mix my grandma's habanero sauce in my baby formula just to get me interested," Hector scoffs. "This stuff doesn't sound that hot to me. I'm going to need some proof."

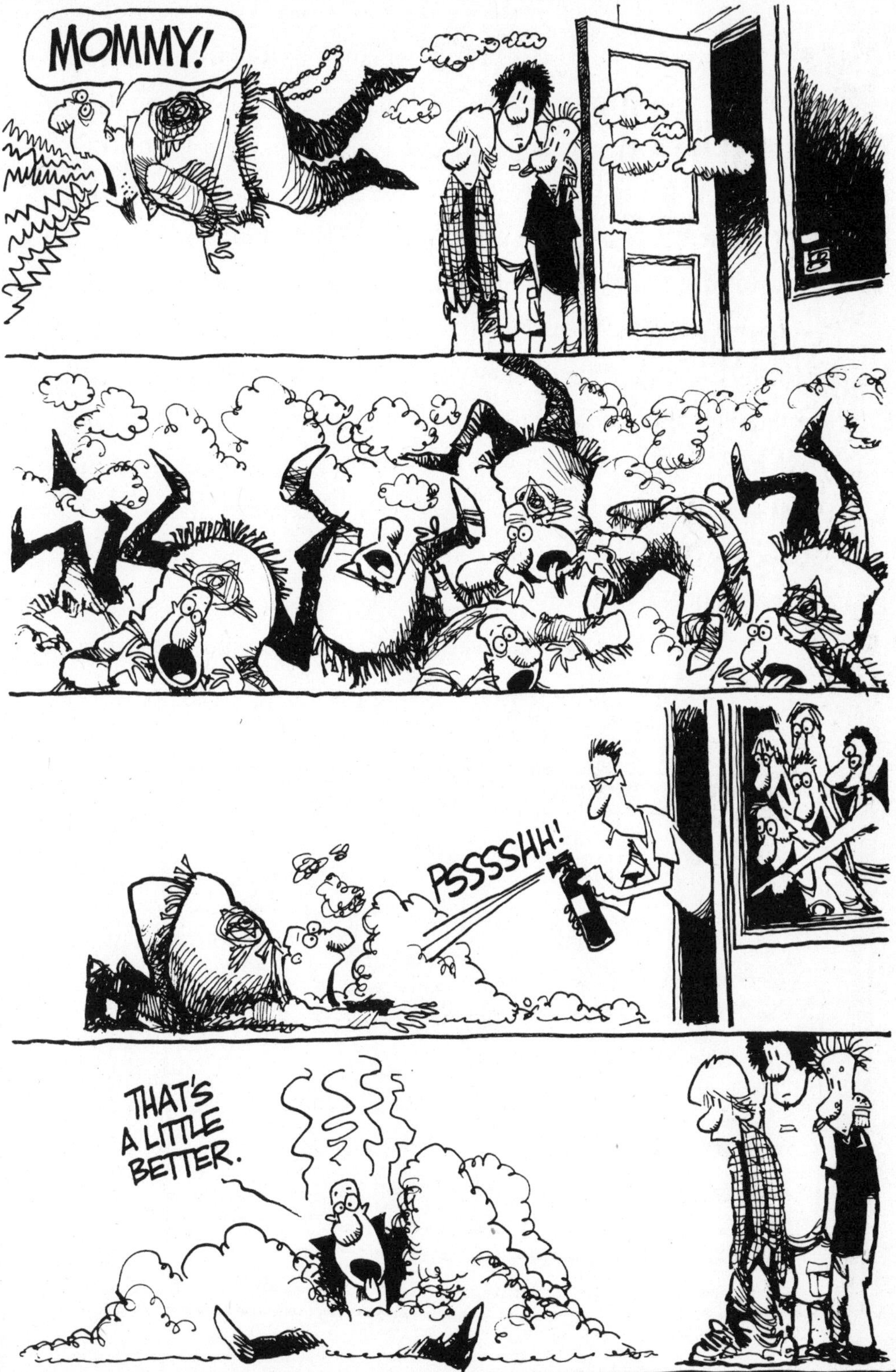
MOMMY!
PSSSSHH!
THAT'S A LITTLE BETTER.

As proof goes, that's pretty convincing, if you ask me. A demonic smile spreads across Hector's face.

"I need a snack," he says, and leads us inside. I look back and see the guy in the leather vest scraping his tongue across the gravel parking lot. This could be interesting.

Inside the restaurant, hanging above a bored-looking cashier, is a piece of plywood with the same flame-butted bear from that amazing outdoor sign. This time he's screaming a challenge: "Finish an entire jumbo order of Scalding Anus Wings in under five minutes and win your choice of a selection of fine products from Chunky's Used Textbooks and School Supplies." The whole place has a real retro vibe, making it seem almost Photoshopped. Now that my eyes are adjusting to the gloom in here, I can see that the walls are covered with photos of some of the victims of Chunky's wings.

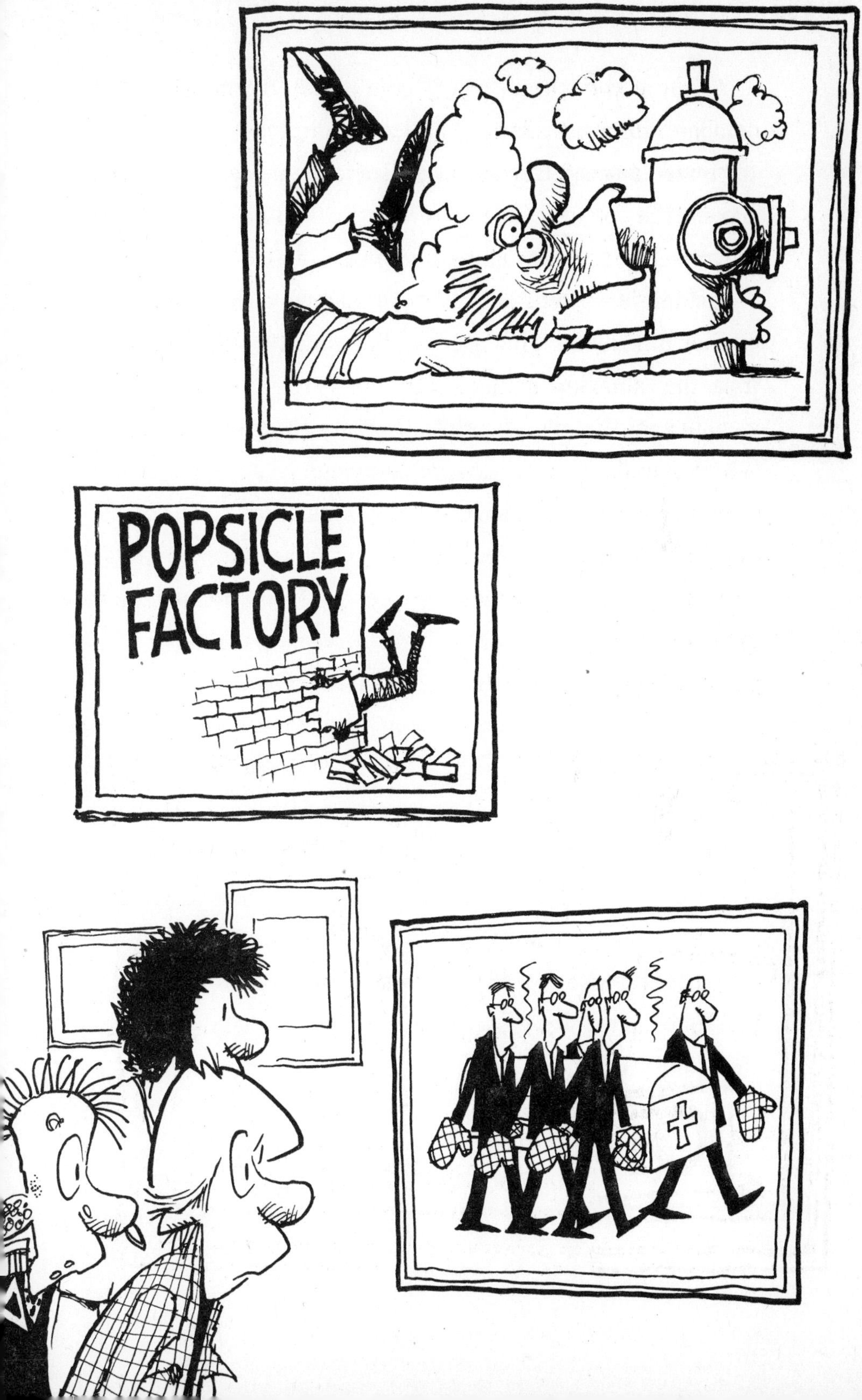
POPSICLE
FACTORY

At the end of the line of photos is the Inferno, a beat-up wooden table with flames painted on the legs and a tripod-mounted camera off to the side. The table is surrounded by a bloodthirsty crowd of rowdy frat guys and over-the-hill jocks. It smells like armpits and chili powder, and I've never seen Hector more at home. He sits down and picks up a menu. He studies it again for what seems like a minute, and then looks up at the waitress, tapping his chin.

"I'm between the egg salad and the *JUMBO SCALDING ANUS WINGS*. What do you recommend?" The crowd erupts in cheers and jeers like a tribe of Vikings. Guys pound on the table and slap money down, betting on Hector's very survival.

A woman at a nearby table shouts, "He's just a child! Show some mercy!"

The waitress stands there and stares at Hector, rolling her pencil between her fingers impatiently. She's either slightly amused by Hector's confidence or anticipating his demise. It's hard to tell through all that eye shadow. She's about my mom's age (somewhere in her mid-frumpies) and dressed in I-don't-care-anymore stretch pants and a green T-shirt. She takes off her pointy glasses and wipes the lenses on her apron, then looks down at Hector again. After a few seconds, she tucks her order pad into her bra, shrugs, and yells over her shoulder to the cook.

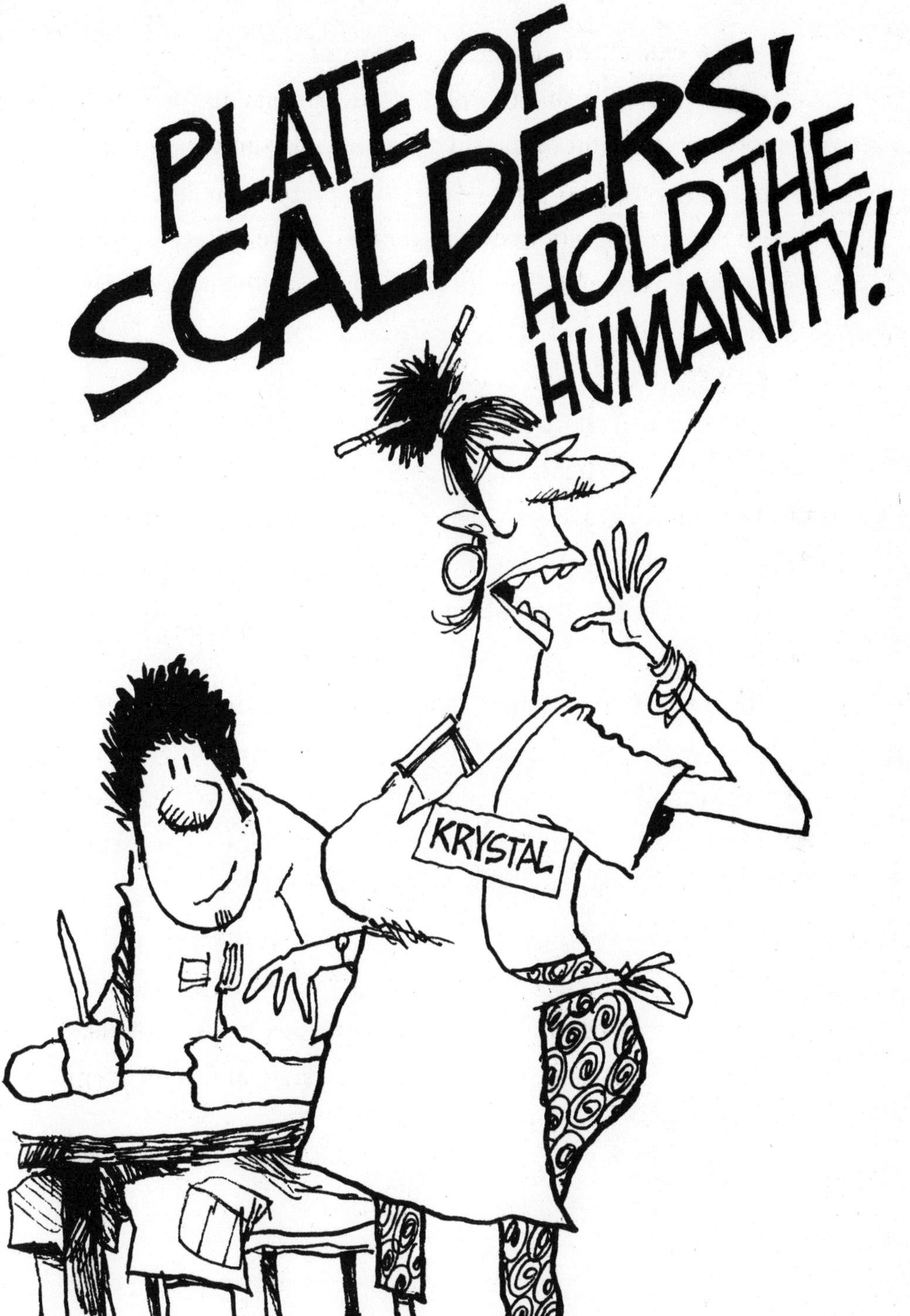
PLATE OF SCALDERS! HOLD THE HUMANITY!
KRYSTAL

Pierce says, "I'll have the iceberg wedge."

"Dude, you sure about this?" I ask Hector, and he just winks at me.

"I got this," he says, and shakes a couple of drops of Tabasco sauce onto his tongue as an appetizer. The place goes quiet, and the regulars all turn their heads toward the kitchen.

The wings are served on a galvanized metal plate that hisses and pops as it is ceremoniously slid in front of Hector with tongs like the ones used to pluck plutonium rods from the nuclear core at Chernobyl. Wagner's the Ride of the Valkyries starts blaring out of the crappy speakers that are duct-taped to the wall. This is Hector's moment.

"For gawdsakes, man, what are you thinking? Use your common sense!" shouts Pierce.

WAIT... DID I JUST SAY THAT?

Hector picks up a wing and, realizing it's hot, flips it from one hand to the other until it cools slightly. He crosses himself and takes a bite. The crowd holds its breath.

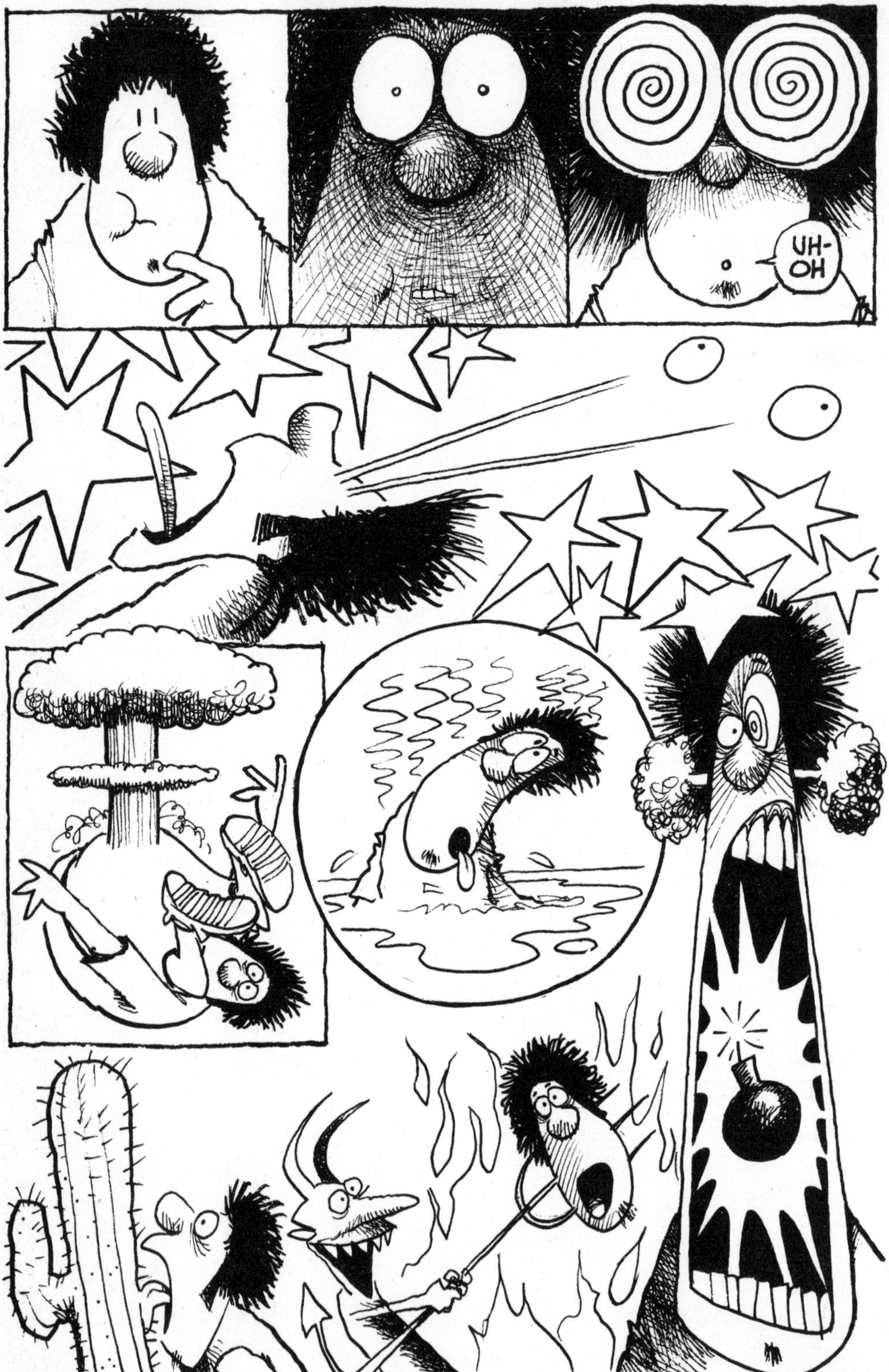
UH-OH

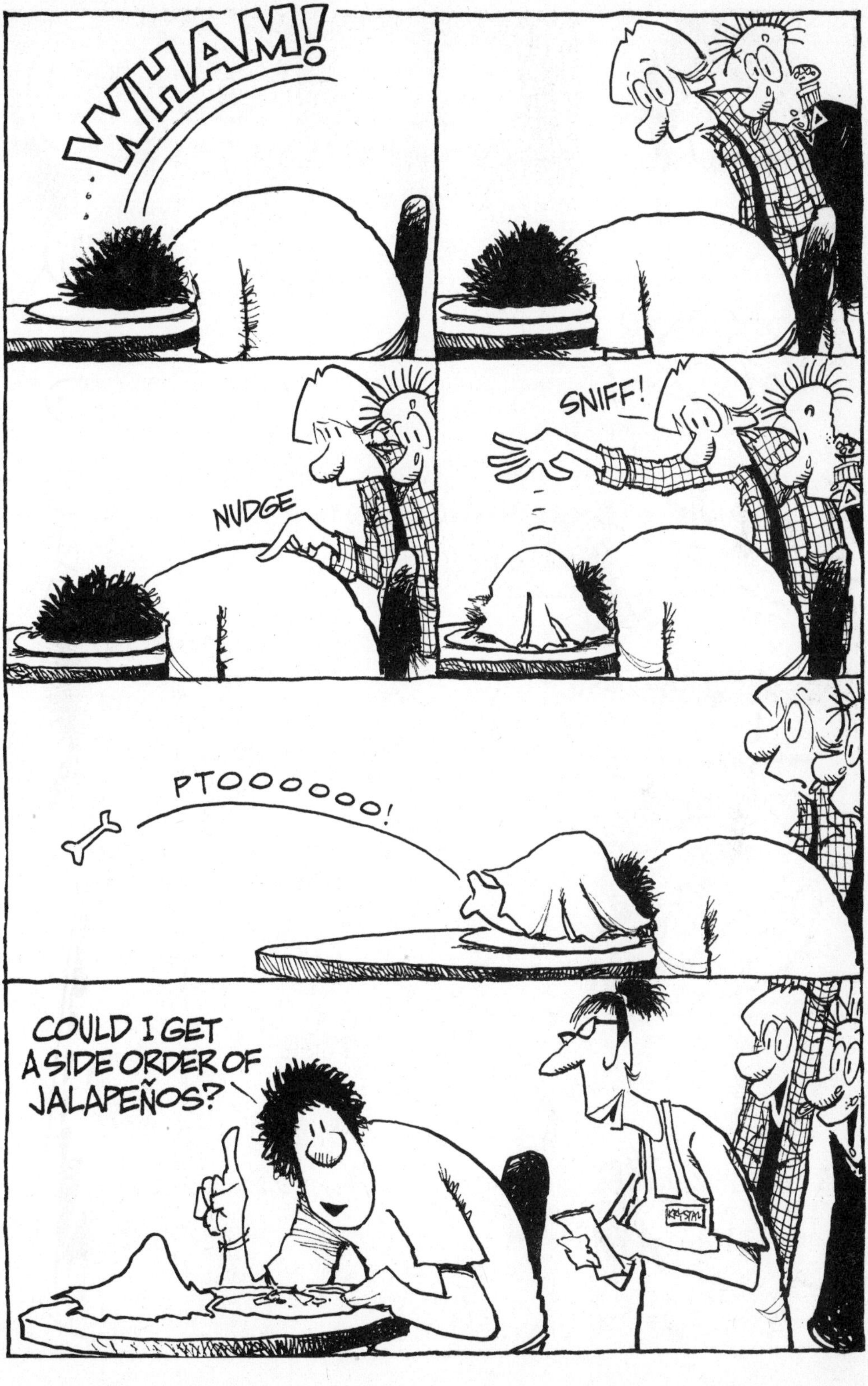
WHAM!
NUDGE
SNIFF!
PTOOOOOOO!
COULD I GET A SIDE ORDER OF JALAPEÑOS?
KRYSTAL

We all go nuts. Guys are jumping up and down and pounding Hector on the back as he proceeds to polish off the rest of the order of wings with style, sucking every last drop of hot sauce off every last bone. Nobody can believe that he is actually finishing a plate of these heinous wings. Grown men ask him for autographs, and women ask him to sign body parts. Hector's face is on the monitor above the bar with the word *WINNER* flashing underneath. It's like Mardi Gras, New Year's Eve, and the last day of school all rolled into one. The guy in the hazmat suit carries a huge box out of the back of the restaurant and sets it down in front of Hector.

"I'm Chunky," he says.

And then he lifts a gnarly-looking machine out of the box and sets it on the table.

"First prize for my new asbestos-mouthed friend. The ShredZall six thousand! Cadillac of paper shredders!" And then, like he could read our minds, he shrugs and says, "Look, I know it's a weird prize, but it's all I got. Maybe you can sell it or somethin'." I guess that makes sense. And as far as used office equipment goes, you could do a lot worse. "This baby shreds paper, paper clips, cardboard, plywood, sheet metal, you name it. It'll turn whatever you feed it into confetti."

"Um, thanks," says Hector, opening and concluding his acceptance speech in two words or less.

Then Pierce jumps in and flashes the Kickstarter screen at Chunky. "We're the guys from the Freckled Children fund-raiser you donated the used grease to, remember?"

Then everybody gets quiet. Chunky sits down on a bench and unbuttons his shirt cuff. As he slowly begins to roll up the sleeve of his shirt, he looks up at us.

"Of course I remember," he says.

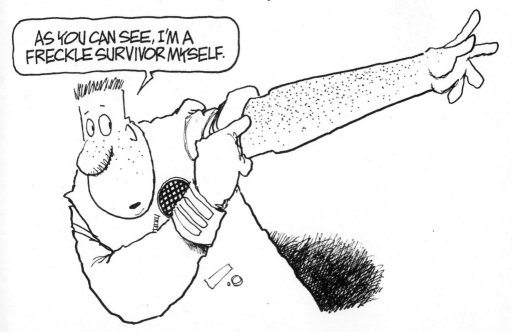

AS YOU CAN SEE, I'M A FRECKLE SURVIVOR MYSELF.

If freckles were stars, this guy's arm would be the Milky Way. Chunky wipes a tear from his eye and shakes our hands.

"Thank you for helping these kids." A single clap echoes through the restaurant. Then another, and another, and soon the place is filled with wild applause for the cause. Chunky hauls his butt off the bench and calls to the cook. "Elroy, get these young gentlemen their oil. They have a job to do."

CHAPTER 7

It feels like I've been asleep for a week. My tongue is pasted to the roof of my mouth with what tastes like a sour cream 'n' onion–based glue, and my clothes are soaked.

"And nice umbrella work, by the way," I add, just because I'm always kind of a snot when I first wake up.

"Screw you. I'm not even one hundred percent sure where we are," snaps Pierce. "I haven't exactly had a free hand to check my maps app since it started raining around Indianapolis, SIX HOURS AGO!"

"No way. I've been asleep for six hours? That's amazing!

We must be getting really close to Sheboygan by now. Let me see your phone." I grab it off the seat and stare at it for a few seconds. Then I look out the window.

"Here's something weird, though," Pierce says. "Did you know there is a Best Buy exactly every twenty-six point three miles on I-465?

"And I mean EXACTLY twenty-six point three. This may be the gas station sushi talking, but I bet it's happened at least twelve times!"

"Um," I say again through the flavor-packed phlegm in my throat. Gross. After a gulp of Mountain Dew, I start again. "They don't build Best Buy stores exactly twenty-six point three miles apart, Pierce."

"No! I'm telling you! I've been tracking this, and every twenty-six point three miles there's a B—"

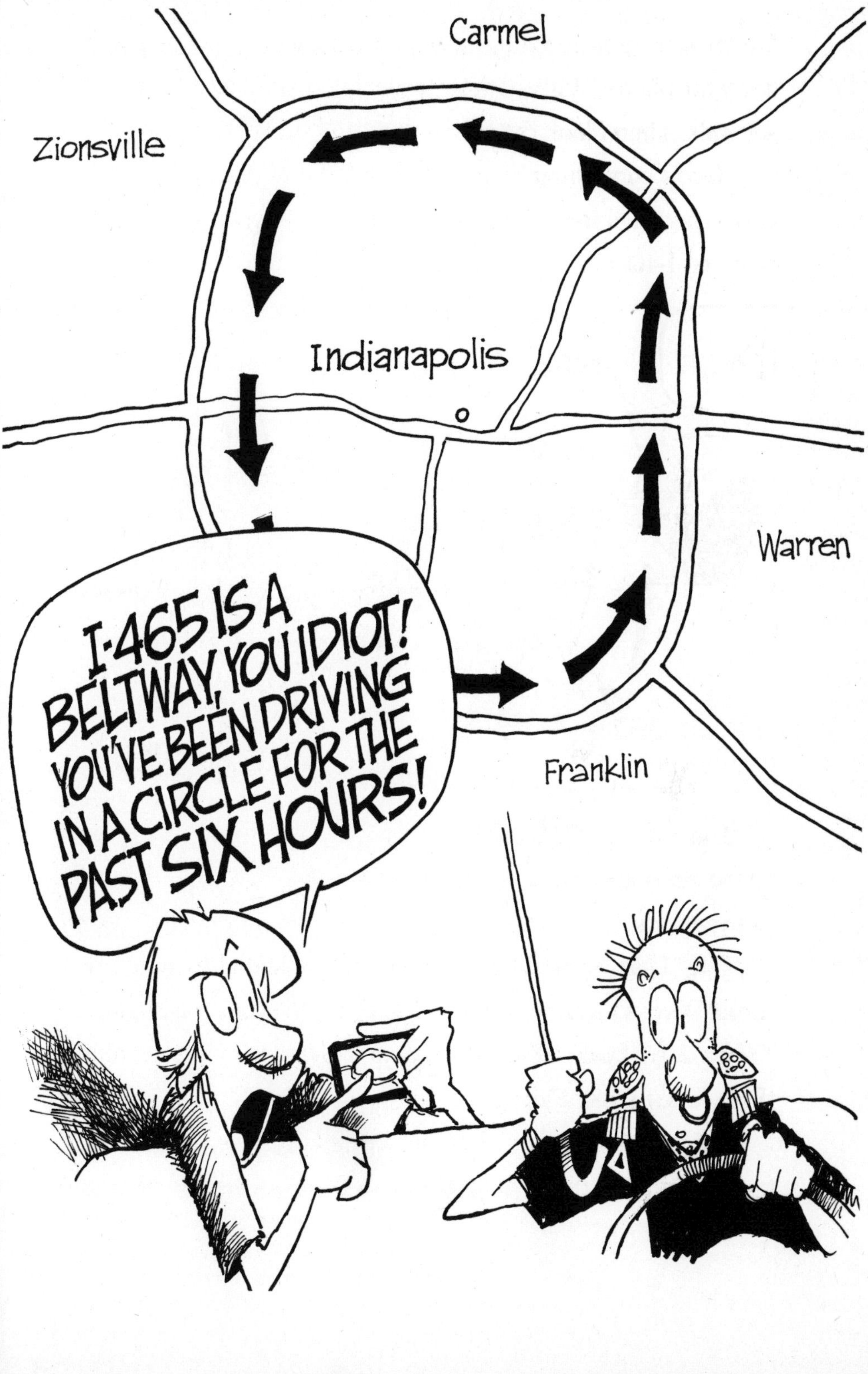
Carmel
Zionsville
Indianapolis
Warren
Franklin
I-465 IS A BELTWAY, YOU IDIOT! YOU'VE BEEN DRIVING IN A CIRCLE FOR THE PAST SIX HOURS!

"Dude," I say, rubbing my eyes, "we are exactly where we were when I crawled into the back to go to sleep."

"Oh" is all he says, and then lets go of the umbrella handle to wipe the windshield off. The defroster hasn't worked since last winter, so when the windshield fogs up, you have to wipe it off with your sleeve or whatever. But you never do this if you also happen to be holding the umbrella that's keeping the rain from coming into the van. Otherwise,

So now we're sort of lost, seven hours behind schedule, and getting soaked by the rain that's now pouring through the hole in the roof where the umbrella used to be. "This sucks," I say.

"Totally," says Hector, waking up.

"Let me ask you guys something," says Pierce, wiping the rain out of his eyes with his forearm. "Are we or are we not on a road trip?"

"Sure," I say.

"Obviously," Hector mutters.

"And we're making our own rules and following no schedule, eating all the junk food we want, *hundreds* of miles from our parents and school, right?"

I don't say anything, and Hector shifts in his seat.

Pierce glances at us both. "Can somebody please tell me what sucks about that?" There's a long silence, and then Hector and I both tilt our faces up to the rain.

This is actually the most fun I've ever had, and I didn't even know it. "I've got an idea," says Hector, pointing ahead. "Take the next exit."

I have to admit that I thought Hector was out of his mind when he told Pierce to pull in to this strip mall, but it turned out to be pure genius. If you're looking for a warm, dry shelter where a few quarters will buy you some dry clothes, you could do worse than the 24-hour Sir Suds-a-Lot in Carmel, Indiana. And we have the place to ourselves. Sweet!

"Hmm-fump-a hmmm fump-a bumbumfump-a-bum . . ." The big industrial dryers toss our wet jeans, sweatshirts, and shoes around in circles, and Pierce picks up on the cool rhythm of it all. He starts to play along on an old Tide box, and Hector adds this chord progression in F sharp minor he's been working on. It has a weird, wistful sound to it that for some reason makes me think of Frankenstein. Frankenstein . . . Freckles . . . Frecklestein! Not bad! I spot a pen that's sticking out of a wad of lint on the floor and start writing some random lyrics on my leg. *Freckles . . . speckles . . . heckles . . .* this thing is starting to write itself! If there was ever an Instagram moment, this is it. I snap a few pics and a couple of selfies, making sure to capture the full skeezeosity of the environment. My mom would freak out if she saw this place. I mean, she gets grossed out when there's dirt and soap scum in those little crevices under her washing machine lid. In this place you could base a whole semester of biology on the crud that's smeared on the change machine alone. It's awesome. I start humming a melody of some sort and it actually sounds pretty good. Better than pretty good, in fact. We sound incredible, partly because it's three o'clock in the morning and we're practically naked in a random Laundromat near Indianapolis, but mostly because the acoustics in here are amazing! I make a note on the back of my calf.

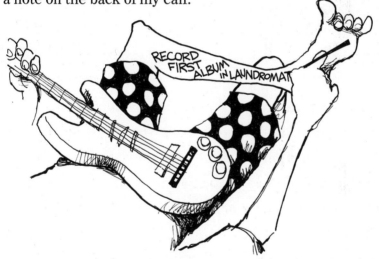

My phone vibrates, and it's a text from Sara. That's interesting. She usually doesn't stay up this late. "Idea for the Freckled Children fund-raiser: Get autographs from all the A-list freckled TV and movie stars and auction them off." Not bad. Then, "Problem: There really aren't that many. GAWD! Why is this so hard? Luv the pics on Instagram!"

"Never fear," I write back. "We have this thing totally under control." I push Send and then look up.

I see some movement outside through the streaky Laundromat windows, and then a blazing light slices through the dim room, sending Hector and me diving for cover. Pierce isn't as shy, and takes full advantage of the spotlight.

"Hello, boys," a short cop with a bristly mustache says. "Having a little rehearsal tonight?" There's another cop with him, and he snickers. The second cop looks sort of like my dad, if my dad were six inches taller with twenty-six-inch biceps, a semiautomatic weapon on his belt, and a look on his face that says "terminal constipation."

"Yes, sir," I say, way too brightly for a guy hiding under a table in an all-night Laundromat in his underwear at three o'clock in the morning. "I mean, we didn't come here to rehearse, and we didn't plan to be practically naked, but . . ."

"Is that your van outside?" growls the big cop.

"Yes, sir," says Hector. "I mean, no, sir. It actually belongs to both of us, so . . ."

"Where are your clothes, guys?" the first cop says with a sigh.

"See, the van has a hole in the roof, officer, and the rain got us all pretty wet. We decided to stop in here to get dried off. And since it was so late, and there obviously wasn't anybody here, we didn't see any harm in it," says Pierce. That's Pierce? He sounds like a Harvard lawyer. "I certainly hope we haven't caused you any inconvenience." The cops look at each other. Pierce smiles and gets kind of a smirk on his face. "This probably looked like a possible four fifty-nine, but I bet you were thinking a three eleven when you looked through the window, am I right?" The mustache cop kind of chuckles.

"Yeah," he says, looking in my direction. "Or maybe even a fifty-one fifty." Pierce slaps his thigh and hoots. The big cop even smiles a little. What the heck is happening here? The next thing I know, Pierce is telling them how his uncle was a cop in Boston and taught him all the police codes, and they're swapping stories like old friends. I guess we don't pose much of a municipal threat, so after a few more questions and about fifty additional "yes, sirs" and "no, sirs" from Hector and me, we're dressed and back in the van.

"Thanks again, guys," Pierce yells. Once we're out of the parking lot I look at Pierce.

"What's a fifty-one fifty?" I ask.

MENTAL CASE.

HE WAS SAYING THAT ANYONE WITH LEGS AS SKINNY AS YOURS WOULD HAVE TO BE OUT OF HIS MIND TO TAKE HIS PANTS OFF IN PUBLIC.

Ha.

Ha.

Ha.

It's stopped raining. The moon breaks through the clouds and casts a shimmering light on the wet highway ahead of us. Our most dependable driver, Hector, is behind the wheel and we're heading north toward Sheboygan again. The coupon for Dog Tired Records says that the half-price offer is only good between the hours of ten and ten fifteen a.m. today. If I didn't know better, I'd say that they're trying to limit the number of customers.

I look down at my phone and report, "The maps app says that we have a little over three hundred miles to go."

I'm riding shotgun and navigating, and Pierce is keeping all of us supplied with a steady stream of junk food for energy. With Chunky's used fryer oil in the tank and three Red Bulls in hand, Hector puts the pedal to the metal—or whatever the floorboard is patched with on the driver's side. The residual spices in the oil from the hot wings must be good for the engine, because we're actually approaching the speed limit without going downhill. And we're all appreciating the fact that we've slipped out of metro Indianapolis without a felony on our records. Things are looking up. At least they are until the hamster escapes.

CHAPTER 8

She has a point. But then, I was just woken from a great nap by a half pound of hairy mayhem trespassing in my shorts, and that automatically gives me a free pass on speed talk. I haven't known a lot of hamsters (Pierce named this one Lucifer, which seems about right), but this guy definitely seemed to have anger issues, or at least a nasty case of rodent ADHD. Either way, he was fast and equally surprised as me to learn that a human can actually levitate when threatened in the groinish region.

"I just had sort of a near-castration experience, and I needed to tell somebody about it," I say.

"Ohmygawd! What happened?" Sara asks. That's what I'm looking for . . . just a hint of concern from a caring person.

"Pierce brought his stupid hamster along. It got loose and took a scenic tour up my pants and around the neighborhood, so to speak."

HECTOR JUST POSTED SOME PICTURES!

HAHAHAHAHAHA HA HA HA HA HA HA HA HA HA HA HA

WHY DON'T YOU EVER DANCE LIKE THAT WITH ME?

"All right. Never mind. Just tell me how everything is going with you," I say, changing the subject to anything non-hamster.

"Oh! I didn't tell you, did I? D'ijon heard that idiot Connor Mattson changed the date of his party to tomorrow! Can you believe that jerk? I think he did it just to mess with our Freckled Children fund-raiser dance, so, yeah. There goes, like, probably ninety percent of our crowd!" I hear a ripping sound, like a girl taking a bite out of a pillow, followed by a spitting sound, like a girl trying to get feathers out of her mouth. Then Sara sighs. "Sometimes success feels like lightning years away, you know?"

"You mean *light-years*," I say.

"What?"

"Never mind. I like your way better." *Saraphrasing.* That's what I call it when she massacres the language like that. It's one of the, like, ten million things that is so amazing about her. "Anyway, that sucks," I say, changing the subject back to Connor Mattson's jerkish ways. "What are we going to do?"

Sara yawns, and I can hear her pull the covers up around her shoulders.

It's obvious that the success of the whole fund-raiser thing is up to Hector, Pierce, and me now. After just planning the dance, reserving the space, doing the promotion, making posters, selling tickets, soliciting donations, buying supplies, renting tables, baking brownies, and setting everything up, Sara, Autumn, and D'ijon have pretty much dumped the project into our laps. Leave it to them to ruin a perfectly good group effort by expecting the guys to help.

The last six hours of highway between the Laundromat and wherever we are have made me hungry again. I take a picture of the back of Pierce's head just to annoy him and stuff my phone into my pocket. The sun has been up for a while now, and we must be getting pretty close to Sheboygan. "If I eat another bag of anything barbecue/nacho/sour cream 'n' onion–flavored, I'm going to yodel my groceries," I graphically announce. "Is anybody else hungry for real food?"

No need to ask twice. Hector steers the van up the next off-ramp toward a truck stop sign the size of my front yard.

We weave through a canyon of big rigs and finally find a parking space about a quarter of a mile away from the restaurant. Even though our rig burns fast-food grease instead of diesel, and it's probably twenty times smaller than most of these rumbling monsters, we belong. Parking here feels dangerous, but protected . . . kind of like being surrounded by a bunch of smelly big brothers.

I try to slide off my seat, but I'm not going anywhere. A closer look reveals that a quarter inch of Cheetos dust and a few splashes of Red Bull have molecularly bonded my jeans to the rug I've been sitting on. Pierce and Hector yank me out by my arms, and I walk away wearing several square inches of fake Persian tapestry on my butt. It's a look. After being stuffed in the van for most of the past twelve hours, we're all pretty dazed and confused, probably the closest we've ever come to looking like an actual rock band.

With the help of my GPS, the three of us stumble through the rows of trucks, and by the time we find the door we're all starving. We have to be at Dog Tired Records by ten fifteen, which, according to our navigator, Pierce, leaves us exactly seven minutes for breakfast. Seeing as how most of my week-day morning meals are eaten as I'm barreling through the kitchen on my way to school, it seems like a doable schedule to me.

Inside, this place is a beer belly/butt crack/trucker hat theme park. And that's just the people with the motor homes. The actual professional truck drivers look fairly normal, if you ask me. It's an interesting crowd. Pierce spots an open table in the corner, so the three of us slide in and start studying the menus.

"Can I get you sugar plums some coffee?" I look up and see a friendly but sleep-deprived waitress smiling at us. She looks like somebody's mother, except without the half-lidded mom-stare that they all develop after a few years of having a teenager in the house. She actually seems happy to see us.

Hector raises his index finger and says, "Coffee." Pierce does the same, and then she looks at me.

"I'll have a venti half soy, half milk decaf mocha vanilla latte with Splenda, extra hot, with a triple shot of caramel syrup, light foam, and extra caramel sauce lining the sides of the cup, no whip but a pinch of nutmeg and an extra shot of vanilla."

Okay, there's the mom-stare. Apparently "Coffee?" is a yes or no question around these parts. Duly noted. "On second thought, I'll just have orange juice," I say.

"Two coffees and one juice," she confirms, morphing back to her original cheerful self. "Are you ready to order now, sweetie pies, or do you need some more time?"

"I think we're ready," I say. Hector orders the Trucker's Special that comes with its own defibrillator, Pierce asks for (and gets) oatmeal with gummy worms, and I go for six scrambled eggs with biscuits and gravy from the "On the Lighter Side" flap of the menu.

"Comin' right up, baby jelly beans," she says and disappears.

113

My phone warbles and I see that it's a text from my grandma. "Just talked to your mom," it says. "Told her we're having a wonderful time visiting. If she asks, you ordered the Neapolitan ice cream for dessert last night. Be safe. Love, GMa" Is there anything better than having a cool grandma? For a long time I wondered why she and I get along so well, then one day I figured it out. It's pretty simple, really. We're annoyed by the same things: my parents. When I told her that we were going to make this record and that we might need a little white alibi from her, she was all over it. I barely text back a thanks when our waitress slides our plates in front of us. Nice. We may even have enough time to chew this meal.

"So, who's got a plan B if this fund-raiser tanks and none of us gets into a halfway good college?" I ask between mouthfuls of eggs. The food is most decent, and we're all starting to feel alive again.

"The fund-raiser is not going to tank," says Pierce. "It has us and our most awesome vinyl record."

"Which we haven't recorded yet. Or rehearsed. Or totally finished writing, as a matter of fact," Hector points out.

"Listen to Detail Danny over here," says Pierce. I've been watching him pick bits of gummy worm and oatmeal out of his bowl and slip them into the pocket of his hoodie. Then I see movement and realize that he has the stupid hamster in there. No big deal, I guess, unless . . .

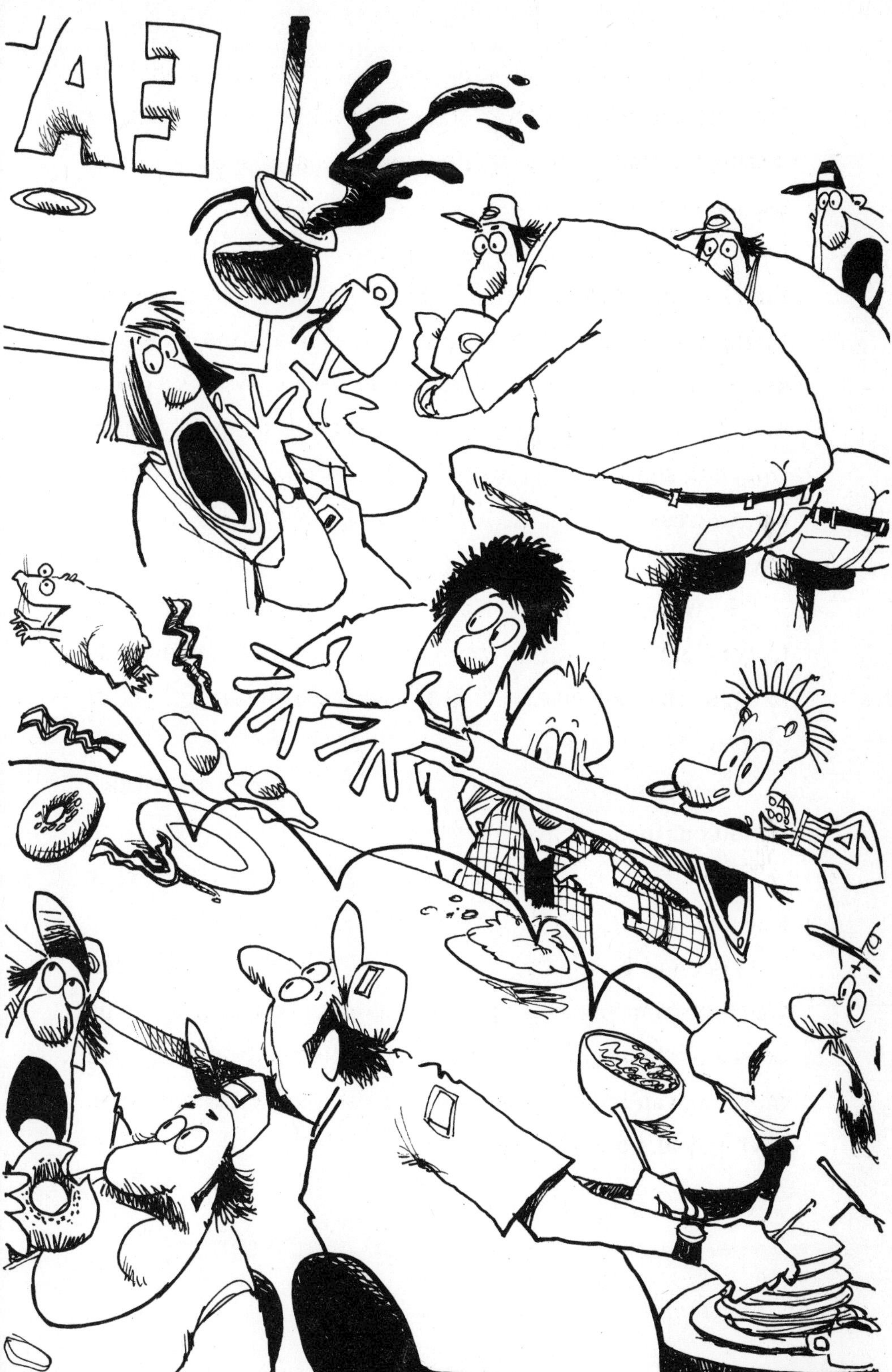

. . . somebody sees it.

After a fast and furious hamster rodeo, and a tornado of apologizing and explaining, I toss some money on the table and we're out of there. I guess the tip wasn't big enough because our waitress winds up and whips a package of beer coasters at me, which bounces off my head. For a middle-aged woman, she has a fairly decent arm. I shove the coasters in my pocket, wave, and follow Pierce and Hector into the parking lot. The restaurant manager sticks his head out the door and wishes us safe travels (which to the people walking into the place, probably sounds more like a death threat), and we duck around the first semi we see and catch our breath.

Pierce scrolls his phone with his free hand—the one Lucifer isn't currently chewing on. "YES! I got the whole thing on video! This is SO going on Facebook!"

"It's almost ten after ten," says Hector. "We'd better hit the road." So we stand up, brush the chunks of sticky asphalt off our butts, and start making our way back through the maze of rumbling big rigs. This must be what it's like to walk through a forest of giant sequoia trees . . . if the sequoias happened to be horizontal and ran on diesel.

After topping off our fuel tank with another ten gallons of Chunky's wing oil (we figure that we'd better use it up before it eats a hole in the barrel), we're back in the van and heading up the on-ramp. Hector starts laughing and looks over at me. "You should have seen your face when Lucifer landed in your juice glass!"

"MY face?" I yell. "Dude, you blew a powdered-sugar donut out your nose!"

Pierce pretends to touch a pencil tip to his tongue and adds in his best truck-stop waitressese, "Can I get you anything else, you baby ducky downy li'l honey-dipped sweet potato mushmelons?"

Between the sugar, caffeine, and hysteria, we're all feeling pretty buzzed, including Lucifer, who's racing around in circles on his little portable hamster wheel like a rodent possessed. I turn on some music and crank the volume up. This trip is getting more rock 'n' roll by the minute! Next stop, the awesome studios of Dog Tired Records!

It's exactly ten fifteen, and there isn't a car in the parking lot. Just a nasty-looking bike chained to a random cement post sticking out of the ground. If the windows weren't so dirty or covered in plywood, we'd probably see that there aren't any lights on inside, either. Our coupon says that the record offer is only good until ten fifteen.

"What do we do?" I say.

"Let's just knock." Pierce shrugs. He walks up to the door with Hector and me right behind him and starts pounding on it. Something is moving around inside the building—probably a depressed raccoon—but Pierce just keeps on pounding until a buzzer sounds and the door slumps open.

Pierce steps inside first. "Um, this is Dog Tired Records, right?"

"It is," says the guy. "And we're still closed. It's Saturday, remember?"

My eyes are starting to get used to the dim light inside, and I can see the guy we're talking to. He's middle-aged—about twenty-five—and skinny with long hair and a bushy beard. He's wearing a Hawaiian shirt that would embarrass any Hawaiian, cargo shorts, flip-flops, and the bags under his eyes are the size of carry-on luggage. He doesn't look that dangerous, so I take a step closer. "We're here to make a record," I say, and then Pierce shows the guy his phone screen.

The guy sighs and drags himself out of his chair, shaking free a shower of sandwich crumbs and cigarette ashes from his beard. He trudges toward the back of the building and motions for us to follow.

"This way," he says. Yes! We're in!

CHAPTER 9

"Did it sound okay?" I ask.

"That," says Ponytail Guy, "was possibly the worst thing I've heard since I crawled under the fence at the state fair to catch a Sting concert."

Pierce looks a little annoyed for a couple of reasons. First, he doesn't really take criticism well (which is interesting for a guy who attracts it like a lightning rod), and second, the junkyard drum kit he's playing on is made from a few retired marching band pieces and a bent cymbal, with a hard-sided Samsonite suitcase for a bass drum. And I thought *we* were underfunded.

"You know . . ." Pierce says as he slams his sticks down.

"Shut up," says Ponytail. "Shut up and learn."

The guy is being a total jerk, but he has a quality that makes you want to listen to him.

"What's your name, anyway?" asks Pierce.

The guy's back is shaped like a question mark, probably from leaning over mixing boards all day, but then he straightens up and suddenly is about four inches taller.

"Fnu Lnu. *First name unknown, Last name unknown.* You can call me Fnu." He starts dragging mic stands and amps around the room while muttering to himself. Fnu makes Hector and me trade places, and then stands in the middle of the room, squinting at us. "You guys have potential. That's not to say it won't take a miracle for me to pull it together in there, but if anyone can do it, it's me."

Wow. That may be the biggest compliment we've gotten since my mom said that our music helped her sinuses drain.

"Where's your bass player?"

"He couldn't make the trip," I say cautiously. "But on the way here I sang the song to him over the phone. He recorded his track at home and then emailed me an MP3 file."

"Resourceful. I like that," says Fnu. He grabs my phone and walks back to the booth. "I'll download it and cue it up. You guys get ready for your first and *final* take. It's almost eleven, and I've got things to do today."

Way back when Hector and I were in elementary school, our moms made us join the glee club. Who knows why parents do these things? Maybe they just figure that emotional scarring is cute when it's dressed in a red vest and a bow tie. There was one big holiday concert, and the kid who was supposed to sing a duet version of "Jingle Bell Rock" with me threw up on the woodwinds during the opening number and had to go sit in his mom's lap for the rest of the show.

Our music teacher, Mrs. Henn, knew that Hector and I were best friends, so I guess she figured that we could sing together. No rehearsal, no warm-up, just a shove in the back, and we were standing in front of two microphones center stage with a white-hot spotlight on us. Neither one of us could move. But then I remembered one of the baseball signs we made up in Little League.

It meant to hit a home run or "shoot for the moon," which, okay, never even came close to happening, but it was really cool to a have a signal for it anyway. When Mrs. Henn started playing the intro, I knew what had to be done, so I just gave Hector the signal.

Needless to say, we tore the place up, and Mrs. Henn retired midyear.

"Rolling tape," says Fnu from the booth. I look over at Hector, and he shoots for the moon. Yeah. We got this.

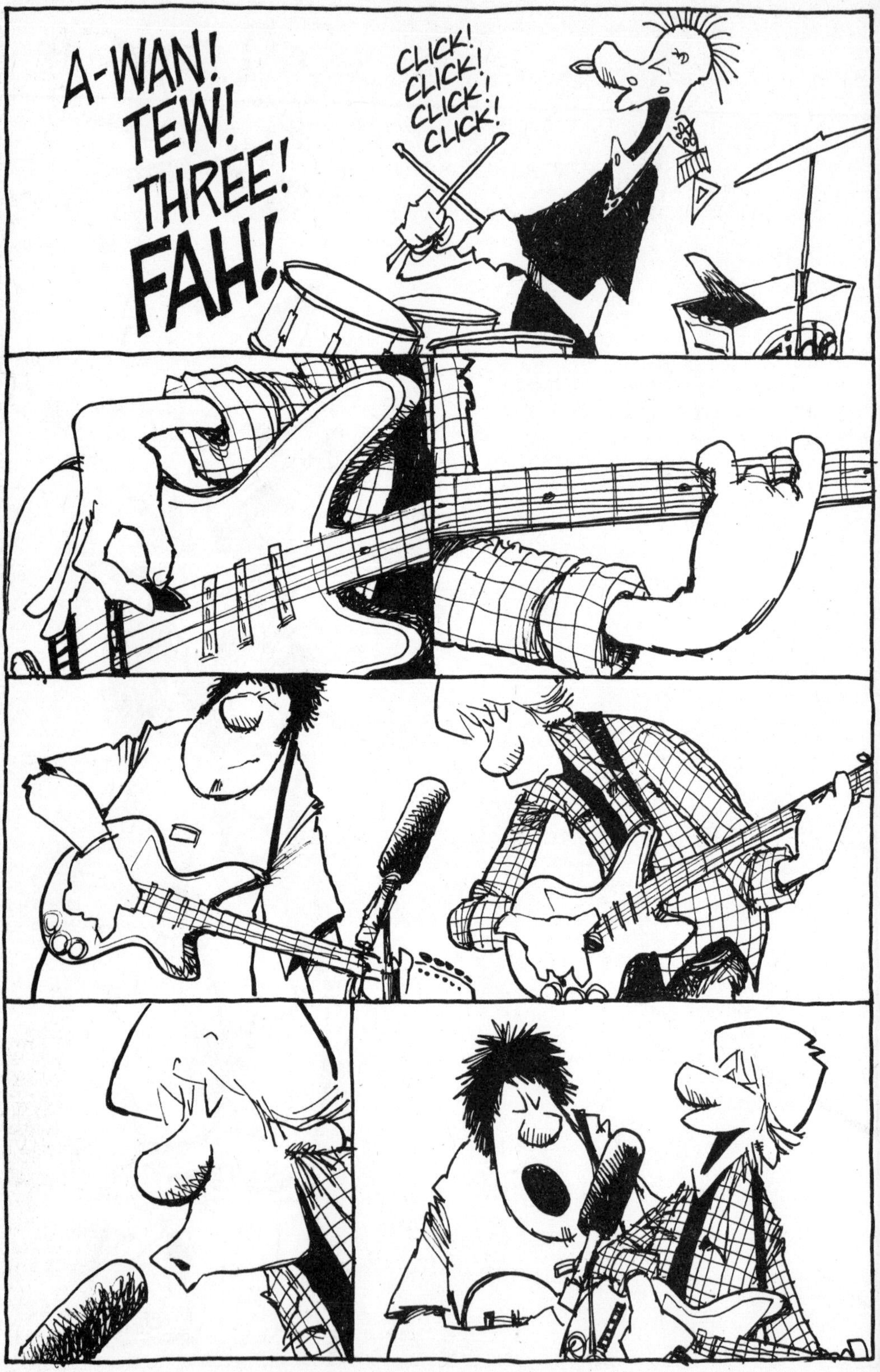
A-WAN! TEW! THREE! FAH!
CLICK! CLICK! CLICK! CLICK!

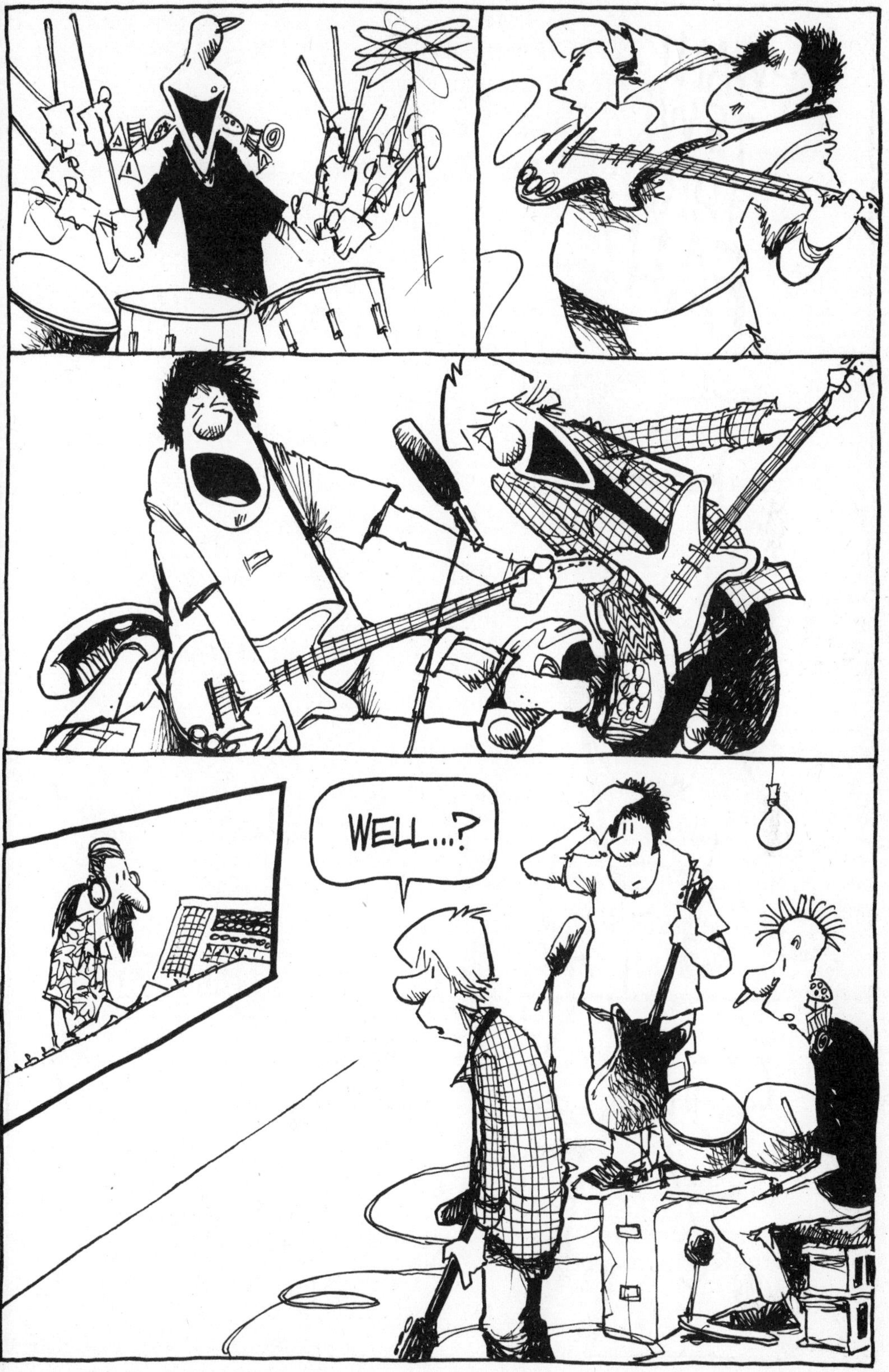
WELL...?

We don't even wait for an answer.

"NAILED IT," yells Pierce.

You know how it feels when you hit a grand slam or a killer tennis shot, or even ace a multiple-choice test? Me either, but this is probably like that. We're giving each other high fives and jumping around the studio like a bunch of idiots. Pierce even kisses his bass drum/suitcase, and I text Tim to let him in on the celebration. "Dude," I text. "Awesome session." And then I add, "We killed it like your uncle's roaches," and press Send. As I'm putting my guitar back in the case, Fnu flicks on the speaker and says, "Congratulations. The hard drive failed. I guess you'll get a second take after all. Stand by."

As Sara would say, "It's so quiet in here, you could hear a jaw drop." Pierce, Hector, and I just stand there staring at one another for a while. There's nothing really to do but tune up and go again, so we do, and it's good. Not killer good, like the first take, but it'll do. Oh, well . . . there will always be other once-in-a-lifetime performances.

A few hours later, Hector is asleep in the van, and I'm sharing a victory box of graham crackers and bean dip with Pierce while we watch storm clouds build over the lake. Sheboygan looks like a pretty cool place, if you don't count this parking lot around Dog Tired Records. But if the crud, weeds, trash, and decay were scraped away, even this dump would have a certain charm to it.

The side door of the building falls open—literally—with a thud. Fnu mumbles something about the door not being right since Meat Loaf knocked it off its hinges trying to get to the lunch wagon. He picks it up, props it against the wall, and calls us over. We all gather around, looking at the cool silvery disc in his hands.

"This is your stamper disc. Don't scratch it. We never give these things to the customer, but since my boss is both understanding and also not here at the moment, I'm making an exception."

He's holding the stamper by the edges really carefully, like it's made out of silver or something.

"What's a stamper disc and what are we supposed to do with it?" Hector asks.

Fnu rolls his eyes and heads back into the building with us right behind. "The stamper is a negative mold of your record. You press it against warm vinyl to make a record, you idiots."

"And that isn't occurring now because . . ." I say.

Fnu waves an arm toward a hulking, wacky-looking piece of machinery that occupies most of the room. "A Chinese company bought all of our equipment and is going to use it to make cell phones or something," he says. "Anyway, it's time for me to move on. Make your own records. The coupon lied. Deal with it." Fnu picks up his backpack from a dusty corner of the building and heads for the door.

"No charge, by the way. Not even for the miracle I just performed in the mixing booth. You should be proud. That was the freakiest tune I've recorded since Enya went reggae. Fitting that it's the last." He's unchaining his bike from the cement post and I step forward.

"C'mon, man! How are we supposed to make our own records?"

Fnu hangs the bike chain around his neck and throws his leg over his junkyard bike. "How? Figure it out is how."

SQUISHING WARM VINYL INTO A MOLD... IT AIN'T ROCKET SCIENCE!

My phone starts vibrating again. It's been doing that about every ten minutes for the last few hours, but since it was my mom calling, I've been letting it go to voice mail. It says she's left eighteen messages, so I figure that it might be wise to answer this time. I wonder if she's pissed.

"Mom. Mom. Mom. Mom. Mom. I'm sorry. I didn't pick up earlier because I was busy, um, doing stuff with Grandma. Yeah, like eating Neapolitan ice cream and stuff. Yum!" Man, even I'm not believing me. "You want to talk to her? Um, she can't now because she, uh . . ."

" . . . is playing bingo! Yeah. It's a madhouse!" I wave at Hector to join in. "What? I can hardly hear you, Mom."

I cover my other ear so I can hear better, and my mom says, "Okay, Jeremy. We'll discuss this later. Your father and I have to leave for the award ceremony now. Tell Grandma that I'll call her tomorrow. Oh, and tell Pierce that the *I* numbers only go from sixteen to thirty."

I disconnect, and we all collapse against the side of the van, laughing the way you do when you realize that you probably just got away with something big. After a while the laughing dies down, and then somebody sighs. This is like the turducken of feelings: incredible relief stuffed with remorse, stuffed with overpowering guilt. We're three hundred fifty miles, a hundred records, and a web of lies away from home. I feel a raindrop splash on the end of my nose. We're all quiet for a minute, then Hector looks over at me and says, "You know we're going to hell, right?"

"Yeah," I say.

CHAPTER 10

We drain the last of the Chunky's chicken oil into the fuel tank as mid-afternoon squats down on Sheboygan. Ordinarily, eighty gallons of oil would have taken us a couple of thousand miles or more (with a good tailwind), but Pierce's stupid hamster chewed through the bungee cord that was holding it upright, and the whole thing dumped over. We didn't discover it until just a while ago, and it's taken me almost an hour to unload the van and squeegee the spilled oil through the rust holes in the floor. Just when you think your life can't get any worse, some cosmic force turns up the suckage. Hector and I start cleaning up the last piles of empty snack bags, while Pierce stands there, staring into the back of the van. My grandma's Pilates machine, once buried under several boxes of nacho cheese whatnot has been exhumed and sits strapped in the middle of the floor. Pierce slides the padded bed of the thing back and forth, muttering something to himself and scribbling notes on his arm. He seems pretty into it, so I just concentrate on jamming all this stuff into the Dumpster. Then I hear the van's goofy little Looney Tunes horn honking.

Sure. Why not? Maybe we'll run across a press-your-own-records store on the way to my grandma's house. It's my turn to drive, so I climb in and get situated. As I'm adjusting the rearview mirror, I hear Pierce and Siri making plans in the back, so I guess he's the navigator. I roll the van out to the corner of Burned and Defeated and wait for instructions. Pierce keeps messing with his phone in the backseat, so I try to start a civil conversation about the crapitude of our lives.

"Anybody know of a good warm vinyl shop nearby? Because maybe they have a drive-thru window that we could just pull up to and—"

"Turn left," barks Pierce. Call me old-fashioned, but I find it extremely rude when someone talks while I am pouring out a serious downer on everyone around me.

"Good idea," I say, hunching over the wheel. "I was just thinking that what we need right now is a ten-gallon barrel of multicolored paper clips."

"Just turn," Pierce says, and despite the lessons I've learned from three years of friendship with an impulsive maniac drummer and his underdeveloped prefrontal cortex, I do.

It's raining pretty hard by the time Pierce waves us over to pick him up at the curb in front of Staples. Hector leans back and opens the rear door, and Pierce tumbles into the backseat carrying a George Foreman Lil' Georgie Portable Deluxe Electric Hot Plate and a half-dozen bags of random supplies that almost crush Lucifer, who was chilling in an open plastic jug of turkey jerky. He gives Pierce the hamster stink eye and Pierce apologizes, "Sorry, sorry, sorry."

Okay, maybe that is a good sign. I yank at the bag of kettle corn that we had jammed into the hole to waterproof the roof. It was sort of working, but the rain is coming down harder and I'm hungry again, so I shove the Hello Kitty umbrella through it and duct-tape it into place. Much better. Now we look just the right amount of insane. Hector grabs a handful of my kettle corn, turns around in his seat, and says to Pierce, "I found a Home Depot three-tenths of a mile away, like you asked me to. Maybe they're still running their buy-a-skid-of-mulch-and-get-an-Elmo-glow-in-the-dark-hairband special."

Twenty minutes go by, and Pierce emerges from Home Depot pushing a squeaky orange flatbed cart loaded with a huge battery, an industrial hole punch, and more rolls of duct tape. We have to rearrange some junk food boxes to get everything into the van and I'm getting a little peeved. I lock eyes with Pierce before cramming him in like a Tokyo subway rider, and he meets my stare.

I point the van toward I-43 and start doing the math. If we hit every light, we're about six hours to Serene Surroundings, Grandma's retirement village. Figuring four to five minutes to deliver the Pilates machine, use the bathroom, answer her questions about how I'm doing, and meet all her friends, we should beat my mom and dad home by at least a couple of hours. I'm beginning to breathe a little easier when Pierce shouts out, "Stop! That's it! Pull into this pizza joint!"

"Pierce! It's getting late!" I yell. "Absolutely n—"

Ordinarily I'd say that I'm as hungry as the next guy, but the guy next to me is Hector. The dude burns more calories sitting in a chair than most people do in an hour on a spin bike. I'm clearly outnumbered here, so I hit the blinker and reluctantly pull in to the You Wanna Pizza This? parking lot. While Hector and Pierce pile into the restaurant, I stew in the car and watch a parade of big doughy Wisconsinites come and go, licking pepperoni grease off their meaty fingers. A few cross the parking lot and line up at the fried cheese curd cart and others duck into the hot donuts shack next door. Which reminds me . . .

"Dude, you'll love it," says Hector, handing me a pizza box through the driver's-side window. "It's the Swine Lover's Special. Bacon, sausage, ham, and pulled pork, and they give you a little plastic lard bucket to drain the excess fat into. I got the Jumbo Dairy Land for myself, with nineteen cheeses and the lime Jell-O casserole dipping sauce."

"What did Pierce get?"

The restaurant door swings open and Pierce comes out backward, carrying a swaying tower of empty pizza boxes.

Whatever. I just find the highway and spend the next two hours in my own head, cataloging some evasive half-truths that I'll need for the answers to the questions that I'll be pelted with when I get home. It's just getting dark when I spot Killian Street. It's in a normalish-looking neighborhood full of sturdy Wisconsiny houses and one picked-over yard sale. I pull over to the curb at 1043, and a guy with bright red cheeks wearing a pair of tortured Dockers sets a heavy-looking box down.

I am not fluent in adult speak, and really bad with dialects, so I point at Pierce. He opens the side doors and smiles.

"Hi der. See, we're music lovers, oh yeah, and the fellas and me were hopin' you had some old record albums fer sale. 'Zat possible?"

"Oh, I hope you're not pullin' my leg," the guy says. "I was just puttin' dese boxes of LPs out on the curb for da trash man ta take in da mornin'. Der yours free if you want 'em. 'N you can take dat old turntable, too."

"Tanks," Pierce says, and proceeds to cram three crates of the world's most heinous musical crimes into the van. Two minutes and a couple of cheese-centric recipe exchanges later, we're waving good-bye to Kenosha and rolling south again. I try to keep from steering the van into a ditch while Pierce and Hector read the titles of the albums.

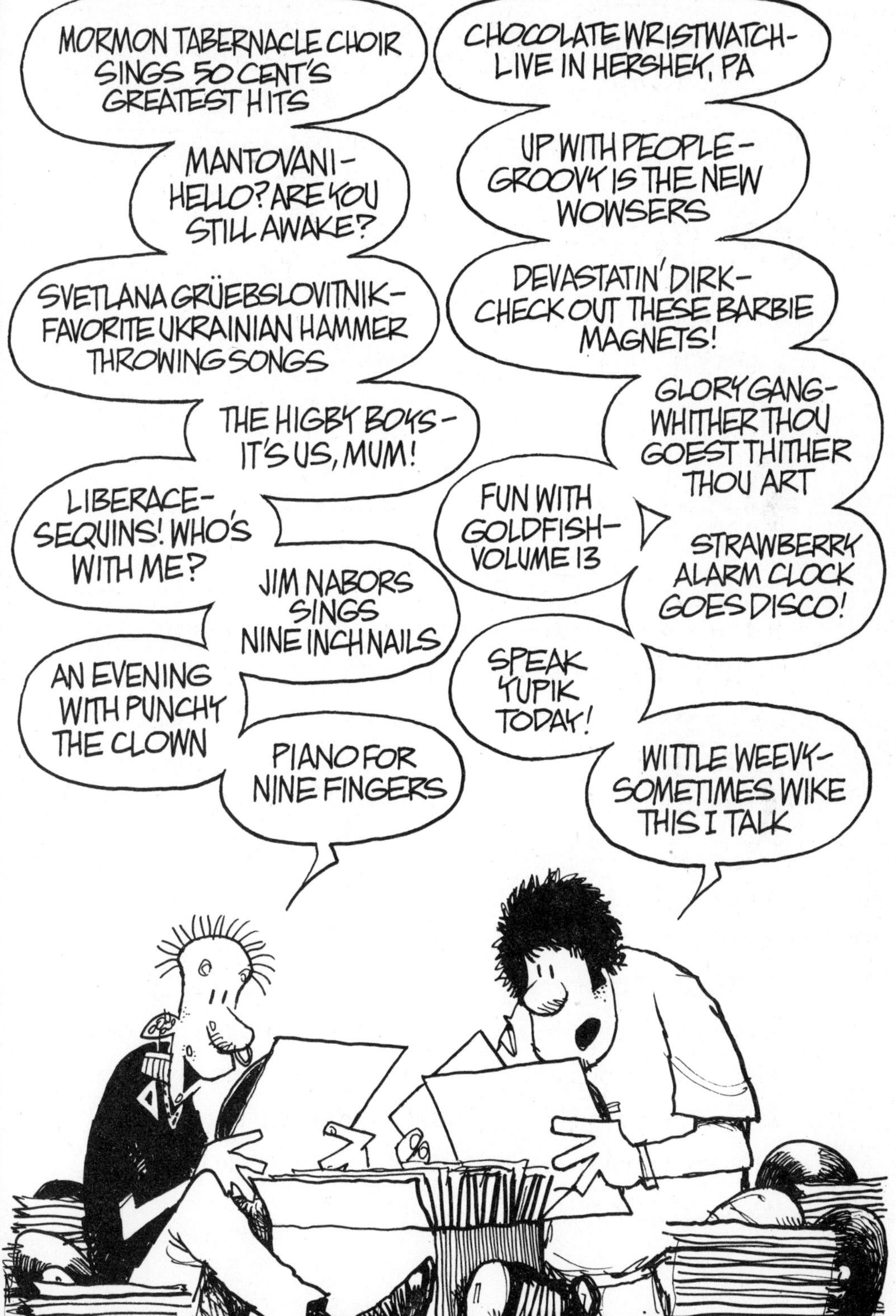
MORMON TABERNACLE CHOIR SINGS 50 CENT'S GREATEST HITS
CHOCOLATE WRISTWATCH- LIVE IN HERSHEY, PA
MANTOVANI- HELLO? ARE YOU STILL AWAKE?
UP WITH PEOPLE- GROOVY IS THE NEW WOWSERS
SVETLANA GRÜEBSLOVITNIK- FAVORITE UKRAINIAN HAMMER THROWING SONGS
DEVASTATIN' DIRK- CHECK OUT THESE BARBIE MAGNETS!
THE HIGBY BOYS- IT'S US, MUM!
GLORY GANG- WHITHER THOU GOEST THITHER THOU ART
LIBERACE- SEQUINS! WHO'S WITH ME?
FUN WITH GOLDFISH- VOLUME 13
STRAWBERRY ALARM CLOCK GOES DISCO!
JIM NABORS SINGS NINE INCH NAILS
AN EVENING WITH PUNCHY THE CLOWN
SPEAK YUPIK TODAY!
PIANO FOR NINE FINGERS
WITTLE WEEVY- SOMETIMES WIKE THIS I TALK

The Walmart parking lot that Pierce directs me to stretches across a vast swath of Wisconsin farmland. The store is closed, and the only occupants besides us are a few random shopping carts and several RVs circled wagon train–style under a tall streetlight. Pierce, Hector, and I are all crammed in the back of the van twisting wires, tightening screws, and generally following the blueprint that's scribbled on Pierce's arm and much of his left shoulder in red ballpoint ink. Pierce sits on the sliding bed of the Pilates machine and adjusts the tension on the springs. He pushes his feet against the piece of plywood that we duct-taped to the horizontal bar at one end and nods his head.

"Heating up," replies Hector. The battery Pierce bought has wires wrapped around both poles and is pumping juice to the hot plate and the shredder Hector won from Chunky's. I press the shred button and the beast growls to life. Pierce grins, then slaps his forehead and winces.

"I forgot the labels! A record has to have a label in the center. Everybody look around for some paper we can use— preferably something round, about the size of a . . . a . . ."

SOMETHING THE SIZE OF A COASTER?

"Perfect!" Pierce plucks Lucifer out of the turkey jerky jug and puts him on his little exercise wheel to keep him out of the way. "Punch a hole in the middle of those with that big hole punch over there."

Easy. I do the whole package in about five seconds. Sometimes it pays to tick off a waitress.

"Then what?" I ask, handing him the stack of punched coasters.

Pierce grabs an Up with People album out of the box and snaps it over his knee. "Then we begin ridding the world of bad music by turning it into good music. Observe."

149

BZZZZZZZ
ZZRR
RRK!
SHREDZALL 6000
TWIZZL
VOLT

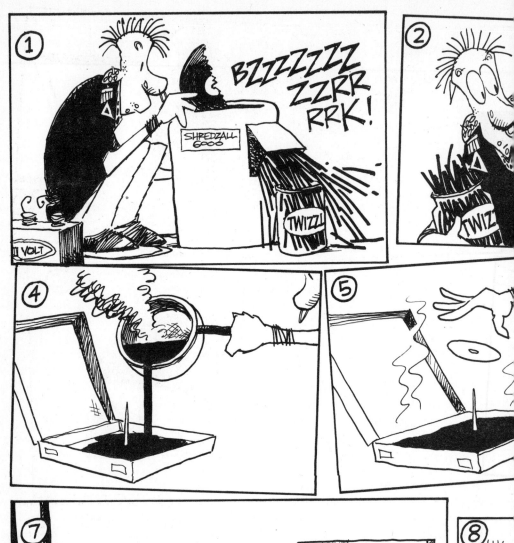

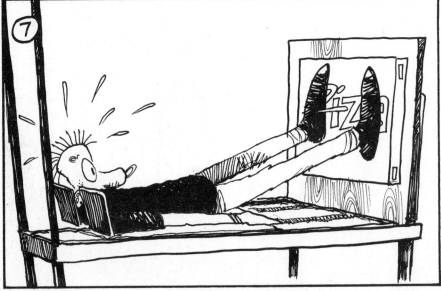

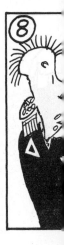

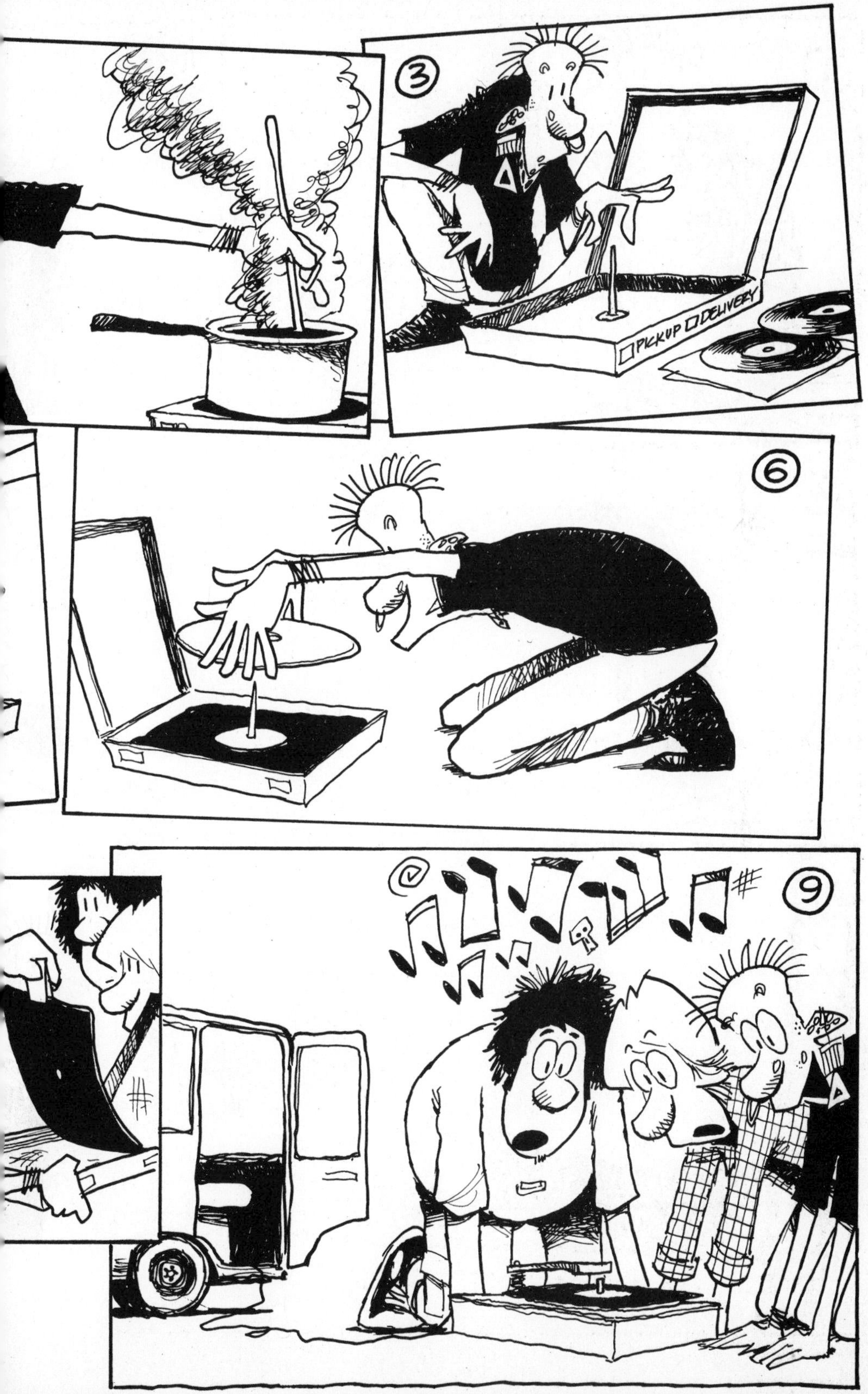
3
PICKUP
DELIVERY
6
9

Oh.

My.

Gawd.

We actually made a record! And it plays! Maybe we're not completely hosed after all. Pierce adds the title and artist info on the label with that red pen of his. I gotta admit, it looks totally Etsy and very, very cool. People are going to go nuts for these.

"Shredded Records is officially in business! Now we just have to make ninety-nine more of these," says Pierce.

"In the back of a VW van while driving all night in a rainstorm," I point out.

"Powered only by sugar and caffeine," says Hector. Pierce grabs Hector and me around our necks and squeezes.

"We'll be legends," he says. "Just as long as the battery holds out.

"Or not."

CHAPTER 11

My phone rings, which I naturally decide to ignore because it can't be important. Nobody worthwhile ever calls without texting first. I glance down at the caller ID, maybe just to see whose name I'll be adding to my Clueless Contacts list. That won't be necessary. She's already on it.

"Jeremy, you'll never guess what," she gushes. I can always tell when she thinks she's giving me good news because she uses my first name in every sentence, like she has to remind herself who she's talking to.

"Let me guess . . . Dad won the Golden Overbite Award and a few old people are twerking on the dance floor?" As I say it, I throw up a little bit in my mouth and then swallow. Eww. Yogurt-dipped pork rinds taste even worse the second time around. I've been to these award dinners before, and, trust me, you do NOT want to see a bunch of orthodontists getting their freak on to eighties hair band hits. Just sayin'. I can tell that my mom is going to start flinging questions about the trip, or worse, asking to speak to my grandma, so I wind up the call. "Tell Dad that I'm really proud of him. Everything is fine here. We'll be home tomorrow before noon. Love you, Mom."

"Okay. Bye, Jeremy. Love you, too, Jerem—"

I toss my phone on the seat and walk around to the other side of the van, where Pierce and Hector are hopefully formulating a brilliant strategy.

"Without the battery," Pierce says, "we have no shredder. Without the battery, we have no hot plate. Without the shredder and hot plate, we can't shred and melt vinyl. And without melted vinyl, we've got no records, the fund-raiser is toast, and we end up in clown college." Pierce is staring at the hamster wheel as Lucifer spins it in another one of his manic episodes. "What we need is energy," he says, and then he looks at me. "Energy," he repeats. Hector's eyes widen.

"Exactly," Pierce says. And then his thumbs are flying over the screen of his smart phone as he barks out orders at Hector and me. "I need both your phone chargers, a roll of duct tape, a dozen paper clips, and a lot of luck."

"What are we doing?" I ask.

"We are channeling Mr. Sporka's physics class—the

section on principles of electricity," Pierce says. "I think I still have some notes somewhere."

"Dude, everybody but Gilbert Merkey slept through most of second semester," I say. "If he hadn't traded me guitar lessons for tutoring, I would have gotten a D in that class for sure."

"Yes, and two great things about Gilbert are one, he's really smart, and two, he likes everybody to know that he's really smart."

Pierce puts Gilbert on speaker and we all do our best not to nod off as he drones on about amperage and current and blah-de-blah-de-blah-blah. After about five minutes Pierce speaks up and says, "Okay. Yeah. You win. That sounds exactly like Sporka, Gilbert. You the man. Bye." Pierce plucks Lucifer off the hamster wheel and gives him a kiss on the nose before dropping him into the turkey jerky jug. "Take a rest, buddy. You're going to need it."

I must be really tired because it makes perfect sense to me that a hamster-powered generator can create enough juice to run a George Foreman hot plate and a paper shredder. I pop another can of warm Red Bull and take a gulp. I'm definitely going to cut down on caffeine after this trip is over because I think I can feel my fingernails vibrating. I watch as Pierce and Hector start assembling our mini power plant. They seem to know what they're doing, so I stay out of the way and offer helpful wisecracks to keep them entertained. Pierce shows Hector a phone app that boosts the output of something or other, and they patch it into the system. It's pretty amazing, really. The whole thing is coming together with ingenuity, random office supplies, and the stuff Gilbert told us, which Pierce scribbled on the inside of his elbow. To me, it looks a little like a big Mouse Trap game, but less tidy and without a guy in an old-timey bathing suit diving into an empty tub.

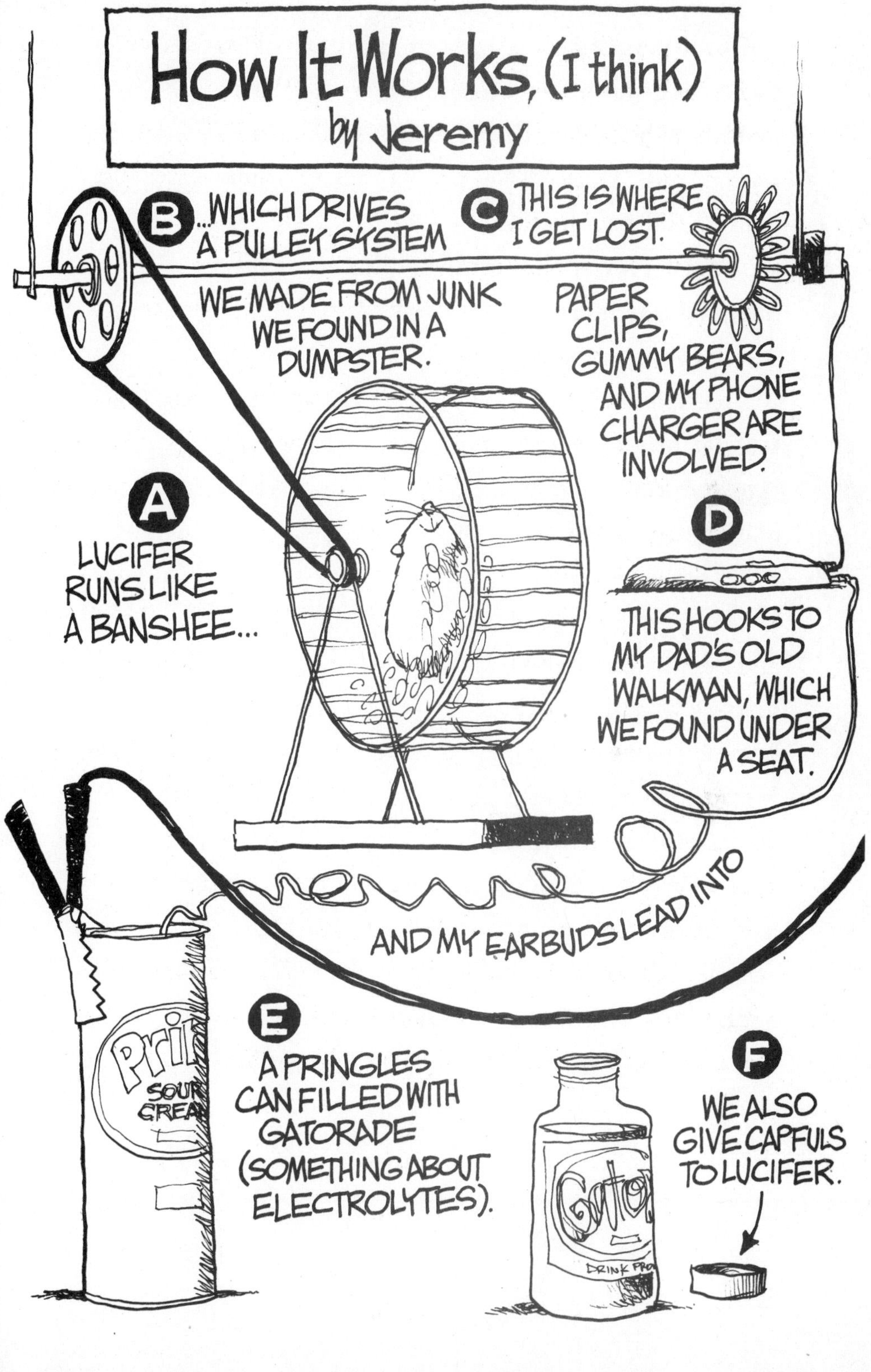
How It Works, (I think)
by Jeremy
A
LUCIFER RUNS LIKE A BANSHEE...
B
...WHICH DRIVES A PULLEY SYSTEM
WE MADE FROM JUNK WE FOUND IN A DUMPSTER.
C
THIS IS WHERE I GET LOST.
PAPER CLIPS, GUMMY BEARS, AND MY PHONE CHARGER ARE INVOLVED.
D
THIS HOOKS TO MY DAD'S OLD WALKMAN, WHICH WE FOUND UNDER A SEAT.
AND MY EARBUDS LEAD INTO
E
A PRINGLES CAN FILLED WITH GATORADE (SOMETHING ABOUT ELECTROLYTES).
F
WE ALSO GIVE CAPFULS TO LUCIFER.

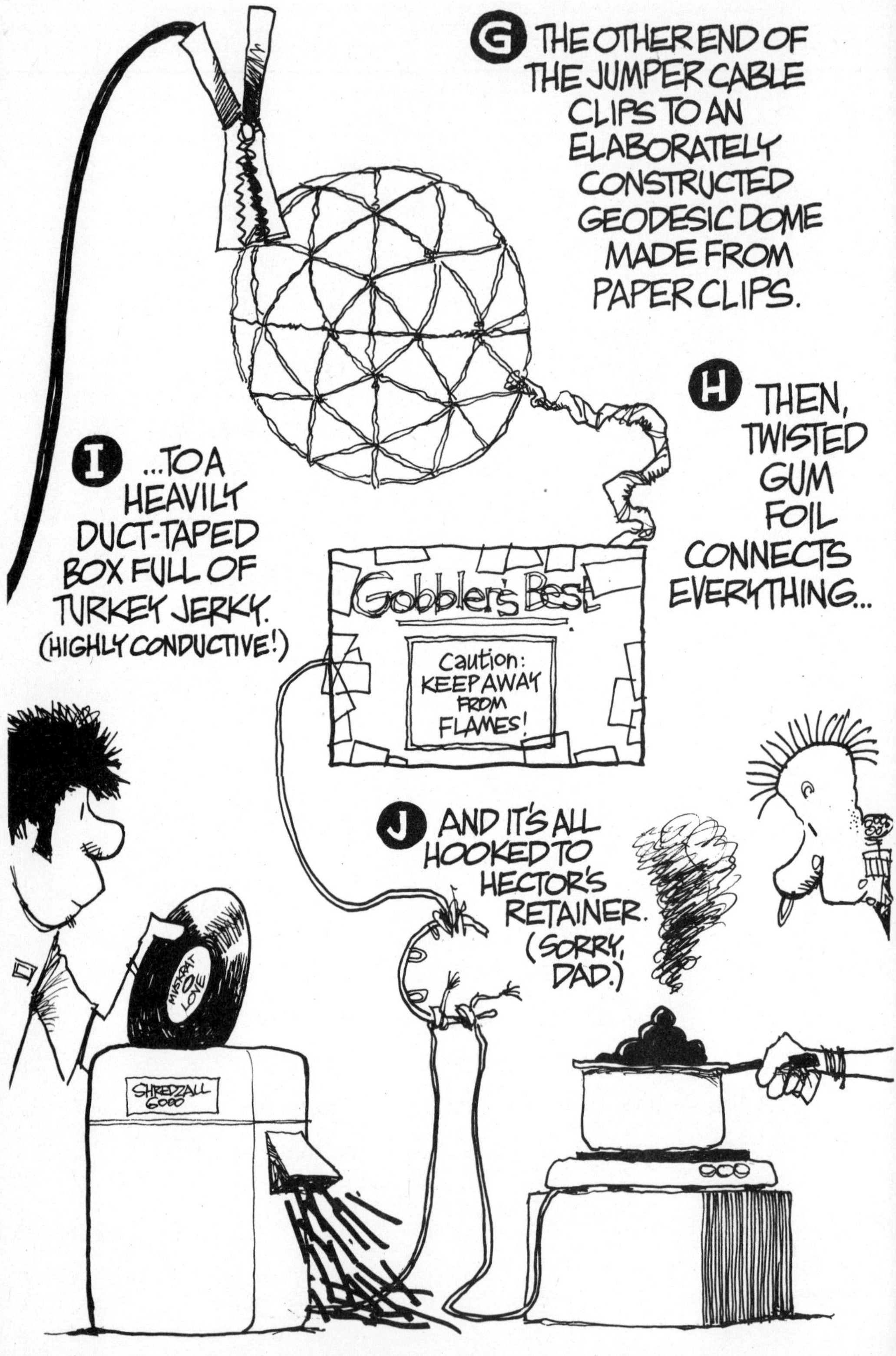

G THE OTHER END OF THE JUMPER CABLE CLIPS TO AN ELABORATELY CONSTRUCTED GEODESIC DOME MADE FROM PAPER CLIPS.
H THEN, TWISTED GUM FOIL CONNECTS EVERYTHING...
I ...TO A HEAVILY DUCT-TAPED BOX FULL OF TURKEY JERKY. (HIGHLY CONDUCTIVE!)
Gobbler's Best
Caution: KEEP AWAY FROM FLAMES!
J AND IT'S ALL HOOKED TO HECTOR'S RETAINER. (SORRY, DAD.)
SHREDZALL 6000

Pierce puts Lucifer on the hamster wheel and whispers in his ear.

The squeaky wheel starts to turn, slowly at first, then faster as Lucifer gets going, until the squeak becomes a constant high-pitched whine. The vinyl on the hot plate starts to bubble again, and we are back in business!

It's around two o'clock in the morning, and since we have to be at my grandma's place by eight, I climb behind the wheel and head out of the Walmart parking lot. Shredded Records is going mobile.

Hector slides an album out of its sleeve and drops it on the turntable, which Pierce wired up to the cigarette lighter.

"A little mood music, gentlemen?" he says. And the next thing I know, we're listening to the Chipmunks doing ZZ Top covers.

Okay . . . it takes the guilt out of shredding perfectly good records once you've experienced the full terribleness of their music. Pierce laughs and grabs the Chipmunks record. He feeds it into the shredder with one hand and puts the next record on the turntable with the other hand. *Pizza Party Polka* gets another howl from Hector, and I crack up, sending a fine Red Bull mist out my nose and onto the dashboard. With Lucifer running his stubby legs off in the hamster wheel generator (with short breaks only for back rubs and energy snacks), Pierce and Hector work together in a synchronized vinyl ballet, turning out disk after disk, while I chew up miles of highway. Before he hangs the freshly pressed records on a clothesline that Hector improvised from shoelaces and upholstery strings he pulled out of the backseat, Pierce adds the final touch.

It's kind of hard to describe the weirdness of making vinyl records with a Pilates machine, a hot plate, and a paper shredder powered by a hamster wheel generator in the back of a Volkswagen van driving south through Wisconsin and Illinois at fifty-five miles an hour . . . actually, maybe I just did. I never thought I'd hear myself use these words in a sentence, but I turn my head and yell to the guys, "Let's just hope the hamster holds out through *William Shatner Sings Barbra Streisand's Greatest Hits.*"

The sun has been blazing in my eyes since I turned east outside Indianapolis a while ago (just half a revolution on the beltway this time, thank you very much). I dig around under the seat and come up with some sunglasses that may have been there since the old guy who sold us the van raged at Woodstock. I try a little spit and the sleeve of my T-shirt, but I can't get enough crud off the one remaining lens to see through it, so I toss them back. We're looping through the identical streets in my grandma's retirement village, which was clearly designed by a disgruntled psychologist after one too many rats-in-a-maze experiments. I hear the shredder powering down and the hamster wheel stops squeaking. There's some shuffling around, and then Hector's sweaty face pops up over my shoulder.

A hundred records in just over four hundred miles. Not bad! That's actually friggin' amazing, so I reach back and get a halfhearted high five returned from Hector.

"What's wrong?" I ask. "We got the records pressed, right?" I spot a beige condo that looks exactly like all the other beige condos, except this one has a skull and crossbones needlepoint flag waving on the front porch. My grandma rocks! "We're here! Time to celebrate!"

"I guess," says Hector. And then Pierce climbs into the shotgun seat next to me. His hands are cupped to his chest, and his panicked face looks like somebody just tried to steal his nipple ring.

CHAPTER 12

"Um, maybe we should let Pierce talk to the doctor alone for a few minutes," I say. Hector nods in agreement, and the two of us shuffle down the long, barking hallway and back into the waiting room. Lucifer was limping pretty badly by the time we got to the vet, and Pierce is afraid he might have developed patellofemoral syndrome from the six hours of running around the hamster wheel. I have no idea if rodents can even get runner's knee, but I wouldn't be surprised in this case. I'll tell you one thing: the little dude has heart.

Hector and I plop down in a couple of the fiberglass chairs

that line the walls. Mine smells faintly of dog fur and pee, but I haven't showered in two days, so the chair might have a complaint of its own. It's nine thirty, and I text my grandma to explain why we're going to be late. Again. She was cool at seven last night when I told her we wouldn't get to her place until this morning, but now it feels like I'm pushing it.

She acts tough, but the two of us are really okay with each other. We can just sit and talk without her getting all bent out of shape if I slip up and accidentally tell her something private or especially truthful. One time I admitted to her that the volume knob on my amp isn't really wonky, I just like to see how high my parents can jump. She laughed for, like, an hour, and then hid in my room with me while we messed with their nerves. It's not like I see my grandma a lot, just a couple of times a year now since she moved to that repurposement village (or whatever it's called when a lot of geezers huddle together in condos behind walls). She and her friends there do old people stuff together, like yoga, biking, and aerobics. They also spend a lot of time bragging about their grandkids, and I assume that's why she's been so juiced about me bringing her Pilates machine over. For these old guys, parading a grandson through the cafeteria line is the next best thing to bragging about their latest gallbladder attack. I guess I owe her that much, so I text her a thoughtful reply.

With all the time it took us to reinvent record pressing, and now this detour to bring Lucifer to the vet, I'm starting to get a little worried about getting back by noon for the fundraiser . . . and ahead of my mom and dad.

"How long do you think it'll take us to get home from my grandma's house?" I ask Hector.

"Fifty-three minutes, according to my app," he says, pulling a sheet of blueberry fruit leather out of his pocket and stuffing it into his mouth. "Give or take a few seconds." Hector has been getting hungrier the last six or seven hours. I can see it in his eyes. Dangerous eyes. It's like looking at a grizzly bear that hasn't caught a salmon for a couple of days. I made the mistake of telling him about the pancakes my grandma makes. The ones she fills with applesauce, pecans, bananas, and crumbled bacon. They're as filling as wet cement, but soooooo amazing. One time I ate thirty-seven of them and almost had to have my stomach pumped. Good times.

A door closes somewhere, and we see Pierce coming around the corner.

"Let's go," he says.

"What about Lucifer?" I ask. "Is it his knee?"

Pierce shakes his head. "No. Hip. The doctor says that everything is going to be fine." He takes a deep breath, and then adds,

Back in cul-de-sac hell, I find my grandma's place on just the fourth lap around the development. The needlepoint skull and crossbones flag is still flying, and she's standing in the driveway, waiting with a huge platter of her pancakes.

What a woman. We jump out of the van, trade a few hugs, and she leads us into her kitchen, or the feed trough, as my dad calls it.

The pancakes taste unbelievably good after two days of chips, jerky, and truck-stop food. The more we eat, the happier it seems to make her, so we keep shoveling them in. Her walls are covered with framed needlepoints that she's done, along with a really lousy picture of a red barn with cows in front of it that I made with a paint-by-number kit when I was about eight. The needlepoint pictures are mostly corny clichés straight off the coffee mugs in the Cracker Barrel gift shop, but I notice a brand-new one conveniently hanging right in front of my face.

"Real subtle, Grandma," I say. She wipes her hands on her apron and shrugs.

"Your dad was just like you when he was your age. He thought your grandpa and I didn't know what he was up to, but we could read Walt's face like it was a large-print edition of *Doofus Weekly*. It was actually kind of pathetic watching little Waltie try to get away with stuff."

"What kind of stuff?" I say between gulps of milk.

Grandma shrugs. "You know . . . missing curfew . . . telling us he was one place when he was actually someplace else . . . silly nonsense.

"More pancakes?"

Hector lets out a painful moan that tells me he's almost full.

"Naw. I think we're good. Besides, we'd better get going."

"Yes, I let your mother believe that you left early this morning," Grandma says. "Why don't you go get my Pilates machine and think about getting on the road before we all get busted?" And then, right on cue, my phone vibrates with a text from my mom.

"Leaving motel now :-) :-) :-) :-) :-) :-) :-) :-)," it says. "Have you been home long? :-) :-) :-) :-) :-) :-) :-) :-):-) :-) :-) :-) :-) :-) :-)"

I just text back "No" and head for the door.

Once we work the legs free from the sugar/grease/vinyl paste that's built up on the floor of the van, the three of us wrestle the Pilates machine out of the van and onto the driveway. I forgot how heavy this stupid thing was.

Pierce and I grab the left side while Hector picks up the right side, and we shuffle up the driveway like three pallbearers at some kind of weird fitness funeral.

"Where do you want this?" I gasp, and my grandma motions for us to follow her inside. We struggle up the steps and take out a chunk of the doorframe with the corner of the machine.

"Sorry," I say.

"Just watch the walls," my grandma says, and then heads up the stairs. "Follow me." Stairs. Of course. We adjust our grips and follow her.

Scrape. "Sorry." *Thump.* "Sorry." *Scratch.* "Sorry." *Nick.* "Sorry."

It wasn't pretty, but when you think about it, two good things just happened: We got the Pilates machine returned and I got a great idea for my grandma's Christmas gift.

After a few more hugs and promises to drive safely, my grandma releases us and we pile into the van. It takes a couple of tries, but the engine finally starts, farting a grosser than usual plume of greasy smoke. I guess this trip is starting to take a toll on all of us, including the van. I whip out of the driveway and floor it.

"It's ten fifteen," I say. "My parents are less than two hours from home, and Sara said the records go on sale when the fund-raiser starts at noon. Let's roll."

I'm hunched over the wheel. (I don't know why. It seems like it makes us go faster, I guess.) Hector is riding shotgun. I slow at a stop sign and glance at my phone screen, then over at Hector, who is staring at his. "Navigator?"

"We're forty-six miles away from your house," he says. "Allowing for headwinds, we should be there in fifty-eight minutes." Excellent. That's almost forty minutes ahead of my parents. All I have to do is mess up the kitchen a little so it looks like I've been home for a while. No problem. My mom claims that I can destroy a room by just walking through it.

10:35 Pierce is checking in with the vet's office about Lucifer, and Hector is calculating shortcuts that might shave a few seconds off our route when I feel the first little jolt. Is it my imagination, or are we slowing down?

Okay, it's not my imagination. Hector looks over at me with a sense of doom in his eyes that I've only seen when the orcs are closing in on level seven of Shoot and Blow Stuff Up II.

"Dude, what's going on?" he asks.

"Pull over," says Pierce. "I smell something." I limp off the road onto a wide gravel patch. The engine shudders a couple of times and then dies. Hector and Pierce rush to the back of the van. I jump out and tear after them.

"I smell it, too," says Hector. This is bad.

"What do you smell?" I yell. "Smoke? Melting rubber?"

"I knew it," says Pierce, kicking at the dirt.

"Knew what? What is it?" I say.

"Indigestion," says Pierce.

"Machines don't get indigestion!"

"Dude," says Pierce. "This engine has been guzzling Chunky's hot wing oil for the past two days."

Hector belches and then agrees. "It's indigestion."

Pierce starts pacing and thinking out loud. "This engine needs french fry grease, and it needs it bad. Who do we know around here that can help?"

"Around here?" Hector says. "As in, the cornstalk, porch-sitting, tractor-infested capital of nowhere? Gee, let me check my contacts."

"What about calling your grandma?" Pierce asks.

"Great idea," I say. "In that electric golf cart she drives, she should be here no later than Wednesday. Look, if I'm not home by noon, it's going to take my mom half a second to figure out that we've been driving all over the Midwest for the past two days. And I can't lie to her."

"Take your voice down a couple of octaves and let me think," says Pierce. And then he climbs up on top of the van and sits down.

I'm leaning against a wheel, Pierce is still on the roof, and Hector is taking a leak in the field.

"Why couldn't this be a potato field?" Hector says as he zips up. "Then Pierce could build a potato peeler out of windshield wipers and seat springs and we could make our own french fries!" I laugh bitterly and plop down on some weedy grass by the field and close my eyes.

What seems like two seconds later, I look at my phone and announce the obvious.

"If we don't get help soon, we're screwed," I say, and flop back down on the grass.

"Unless . . ." Pierce says.

"Unless what?"

"Unless that happens to be what I think it is." And then he scrambles to his feet and points. Way off in the distance a tiny cloud of dust rises from the road. As it gets closer, we can see it sort of looks like a car. Or a haystack . . .

"What DO you think it is?" Hector asks. And then it skids to a stop next to us, spraying gravel and grease everywhere.

I'm not totally sure that I ever believed in miracles, but now I could be talked into it. I mean, how often does a person wish for french fries, and then have them show up in a Buick convertible driven by a guy in a hazmat suit? Not that often, I bet.

The guy behind the wheel starts waving his arms, giving the international signal for "Help! Get me out of these french fries!" Hector pulls the door open and hazmat guy tumbles out in an avalanche of golden brown spuds. We drag him over to a shady spot under a big tree, and he motions for us to give him a hand. Velcro straps and buckles are released, and I yank the hood off his head.

Pierce runs over, gives Tim a big, greasy hug, and then turns to Hector and me and holds up his phone.

"I had one bar of service, so I took a shot. I figured Tim's uncle's house was nearby when we passed the Now Entering the Middle of Nowhere sign."

"You guys are lucky that I was still there spraying for roaches," says Tim. "No way I would get in a car full of fries without this suit on."

In just a few minutes Hector and I have squeezed enough french fry grease into the fuel tank to get the van running again. Pierce has been duct-taping old drinking straws together into a long hose. He feeds one end of it into the fuel tank, then tapes our fuel funnel onto the other end and fishes it through the window. Motioning for me to drive, he climbs

in the back with Hector. We all give Tim one final salute, and
then I floor it.

11:15 There's no time to fill up the tank. This is midair
refueling. Pierce and Hector commence french fry
milking into the funnel, and the oil dribbles drop by
drop down the straw hose, out the window, and into
the fuel tank. I watch the fuel gauge shudder back and forth
between Empty and One Drop Above Empty. The odds of this
working are ridiculous. It reminds me of the game Hector and
I used to play when we were kids. We'd imagine an impossibly
huge enemy force, and then one of us would say something
like, "We're outnumbered, out of time, and the fate of the uni-
verse is in our hands." Then we'd run around the yard blowing
up the enemy with laser-guided nuclear think rays and other

pretty cool ideas. Then I'd always picture a beautiful girl like Sara saying something all mushy and flattering about us.

11:47   I know exactly where we are now. There's a section of town up ahead where we have to go through a lot of intersections, and I can't take the chance of hitting stoplights. Back when I was learning to drive, my dad and I would come to this area early on the weekends because the huge parking lots are all connected and you can drive through them without dealing with traffic lights.

"You guys hang on back there," I yell over my shoulder. "There may be a couple of turns coming up!"

184

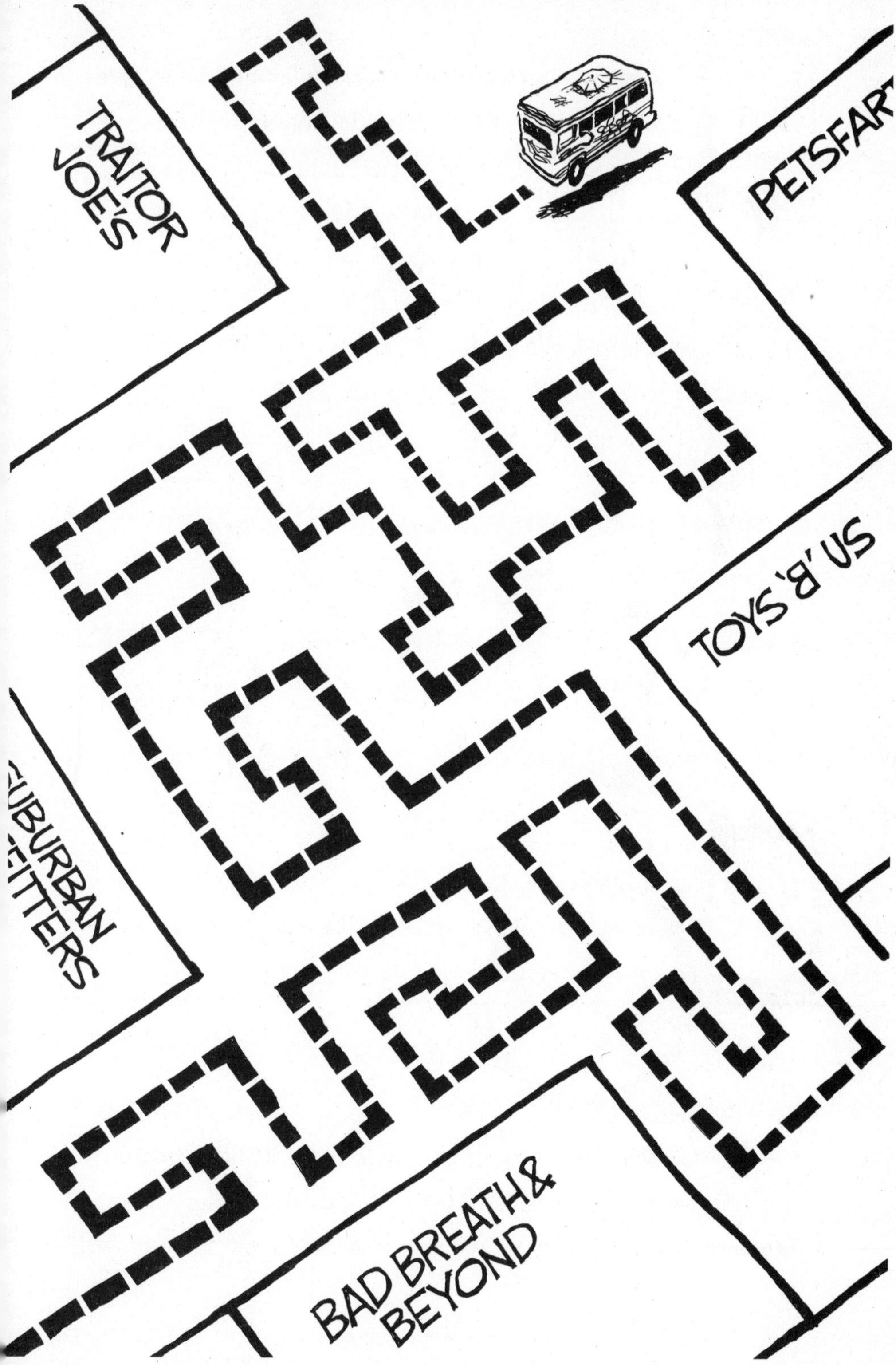
TRAITOR JOE'S
PETSFART
TOYS 'B' US
UBURBAN
BAD BREATH & BEYOND

We pop out of the last parking lot and back onto the boulevard just as the light behind us turns yellow. Yes! The stench of fried potatoes is so thick in here that I roll down my window to clear my head.

"How's it going back there?" I yell. No answer. "Guys?" I take a quick look back and can see Hector squeezing the last drops of oil out of the last handful of fries into the funnel. He looks ill. Pierce is lying on the floor on a bed of wrung-out potatoes, his fingers cramped up from milking all the fries.

"We're out of fries!" Hector says. "Are we there yet?"

I glance at the clock

and then at the fuel gauge.

"Almost! The light up ahead turns red, and as I brake, I notice a blue hybrid two cars in front of us that looks way too familiar.

"Don't. Anybody. Move," I say. When the light turns green, my dad's car accelerates through the intersection, and then, unbelievably, turns into the McDonald's. I roll past as quietly as a veggie-oil diesel-powered vehicle can, and then dip behind a cupcake truck for cover. I throw my phone back to Hector and say, "Quick! Text my mom as me!"

Hector hesitates and then says, "What do you want me to misspell?"

The last half mile to the school is going by in a blur. I lean over the wheel like a jockey on a racehorse. Hector is jumping up and down and Pierce is yelling like a maniac. I come up on the left of a Subaru and pass him in no time. Then I downshift and slip to the outside of the pack. I thread between a Chevy and a Volvo running neck and neck in the middle lanes and break into the clear. Now I can see the school on the left and I make my move. Cranking the wheel hard to the left, I send the van into one of those über-cool sideways drifts and we squeal to a perfect parallel-parked position right next to the sign-in table. Pierce busts open the van doors and says,

Some kid across the street at Connor Mattson's party points at us and yells, "WAAAUUGHHH!" which roughly translates into "That was pretty amazing!" D'ijon grabs a disk and slaps "Frecklestein" on our turntable, totally drowning out the lame DJ that Mattson hired. Pierce was right. Our song on vinyl sounds warmer than the digital techno-crap they're playing over there, and everybody can hear it. One by one the people at Mattson's wander over until his whole party has defected to our dance, leaving Connor standing in the driveway with his mom. People are grabbing records as fast as Sara can sell them. I reach over to give her a squeeze, but some guy waves a twenty in the air and she almost takes my arm off lunging for

it. Right. Business first.

When the last chords of "Frecklestein" fade out, everybody starts cheering and yelling for us to play it again. You don't have to ask Goat Cheese Pizza twice. Sara, D'ijon, and Autumn told us to expect to play a set sometime during the dance, so when they borrowed my mom's banquet table, they hauled our amps and equipment out here, too. With help from a couple of guys, Pierce heaves his drum kit onto the roof of the van while

Hector and I tune up. The whole thing reminds me a little of a video my dad showed me once of the Beatles playing on a roof somewhere a century or so ago. Pierce gives us a count-off and we lay into the first public performance of "Frecklestein."

Thought I found a girl, her smile was superfine,
Eyes of sparkling green, her hair like clementines,
Dancing in the dark her moves were serpentine.
Asked her if she'd be my sunshine valentine.

Lying in the night, her body comes to mind,
Tracing dot to dot pale skin along her spine,
Darkness was to her a fragrant ruby wine,
But the rays of sunshine stung like turpentine.

Never saw it coming,
Caught me from behind,
Took her to the beach,
She spread on calamine.
Kissing in the dark,
She gave her lips to mine.
In the light of day,
Her eyes read Quarantine!

Chorus:
Sun bad! I'm Frecklestein.
Sun bad! I'm Frecklestein.
Sun bad! I'm Frecklestein.
Sun bad! I'm Frecklestein.

Once the summer's rays were warming and benign,
But my love they pierced like quills from porcupines,
Patterns on her epidermis byzantine.
Now I'm in such pain I need an anodyne.
Look it up!
Look it up!
Look it up!
Look it up!

Chorus:
Sun bad! I'm Frecklestein.
Sun bad! I'm Frecklestein.

Sun bad! I'm Frecklestein.
Sun bad! I'm Frecklestein.

Come out in the sun,
Come out in the sun,
Come out in the sun, sweet polka dot,
Come out in the sun and play!

The crowd goes semi-nuts. I guess they liked the studio version better. Or maybe they're telling us how crappy we sound without a bass player, but, whatever. D'ijon jumps up on the van and kisses Pierce tenderly, Autumn wraps herself around Hector, and the party closes in around us, cranking the energy up another notch. Somehow I find Sara and pull her close to me, which seems like an excellent idea until I feel the sharp corner of the cash box digging into my ribs.

"Sorry, but I'm the treasurer, and there are hundreds of dollars in here," she says with a shrug, and then leans in and plants a big wet one right on my lips. "Thank you, baby. We rocked this fund-raiser." I look around the place and it feels good, like the dawning of a brave new world—a world where analog music and freckled children are free to frolic together in the sunshine.

EPILOGUE

Chunky continues to punish customers with his hot wings in Bloomington, Indiana. He received his free copy of the record, played it once, and then removed Kickstarter from his computer browser's bookmarks.

Fnu Lnu left the record business and found work making other flat, round things that make people happy.

Thanks to the return of her Pilates machine, Grandma buffed up in time to place third in the Senior Bodybuilding quarterfinals.

Dad still talks about his Golden Bite Stick Award with anyone who happens to be nearby or temporarily wired in place. He finally decided that he didn't have a weight problem, he had a formal wear problem, and solved it by buying a spandex tux on sale.

Hector's prize shredder occupies a place of honor in his room, and occasionally helps out shredding lettuce for his mom's chalupa dinners.

After expenses, the fund-raiser made almost eight hundred dollars, which, to our guidance counselor's delight, Sara, D'ijon, and Autumn presented to the director of operations at the Freckled Children's Home.

Thanks to his old college buddy who works at an orthopedics company in Warsaw, Indiana, Lucifer's veterinarian designed, built, and successfully implanted a replacement hamster hip. Since it would not have been possible to make the "Frecklestein" record without Lucifer, all but eighty-six of the one hundred forty-three thousand eight hundred fifty dollars of the Kickstarter money went toward the operation. Worth it.

Grandma called the night Dad got his award to congratulate him and to gently remind him of the times his own dad had let him off the hook when there was a good reason for it. Walt took the hint, and in one of the great all-time karmic paybacks, he decided to donate a new odometer to the van, which erased all traces of previous mileage. Dads can be cool that way sometimes . . . even my dad.

Turn the page to read an excerpt from

CHAPTER 1

I can see a bead of sweat clinging to Byczykowski's mustache hairs, and on her it doesn't look bad. Hector is right about Eastern European women being able to rock that look. He used to hang out with this chick named Autumn Solak, who was a total granolahead—meaning she never shaved her legs or anything. The first time I saw her in a tank top reaching up to get something off the top shelf of her locker, I thought she had two cats glued to her armpits. But she was really nice, and really hot, and Hector was crazy about her body hair. Personally, I'm not into that look, but I do admire a well-groomed mustache.

Every eye in the room is on the clock behind the teacher as it hangs on 3:29. And hangs . . . and hangs . . .

Ms. Byczykowski has this weird habit of overenunciating when she reads and accompanies that with exaggerated facial expressions. I guess she's trying to make sure we all understand what she's saying, but instead we all get distracted by watching the afternoon sun reflect off her gold crowns whenever she says "the Battle of Antietam." When she gets to the Emancipation Proclamation I'm going to have to wear sunglasses.

Somebody's cell phone vibrates, and thirty-five hands silently slide into thirty-five backpacks to check to see if it was theirs. It wasn't mine, and when I reach down to put my phone back, I notice a mouse-sized dust bunny rolling around under my desk. I watch it kind of randomly rock back and forth for a second, then rise slightly upward before it vaporizes from the wind force of thirty-five American History books simultaneously slamming shut.

It's 3:30 and the classroom doors burst open, creating hallway-wide rivers of humanity that roll through the building, around corners, and cascade down stairwells toward the outside doors.

Which is cool unless, like me, your last class happens to be on the first floor and your locker is on the third. I twist, spin, duck, and juke my way through the crowd until I finally make it to the first landing.

Pasting myself against the wall reduces drag as I gasp for air and watch the endless flow of studentage rush by. It's like standing on the edge of a freeway, only a lot more dangerous and about ten times louder. I'm serious. If you get near a group of cheerleaders on game day or in the vicinity of the Drama Club when one of them has a cute new pair of shoes, it can make your ears bleed.

Sensing a break in the flow, I dart in and hook my elbow around the metal handrail, and lowering my head, I push

4

upward through the crowd one determined step at a time. The key is not to lose hope. There's this story of a kid who did give up during a cross-grain stairway rush like this. They found tiny pieces of his backpack downstream in the metal shop and his shoes lodged under the vice principal's Prius.

I am not about to end up there, so I turn my focus inward and concentrate on my breathing as I fight against the current. Except for me the current isn't white water; it's elbows and saxophone cases and the enormous armloads of books carried by the simple freshmen who are either too insecure to use their lockers or too clueless to care about the hazard they present. Can't they see them- selves? What is the advantage of carrying everything you own everywhere you go? Is this a school or a refugee camp? As I turn the corner I drift farther toward the middle of the stream. Experience has taught me that this is the spot where the jocks hulk in the eddies and swat at the vulnerable with their bearlike paws, feeding on the weak and unfortunate.

And then suddenly the crowd is gone and I'm moving freely. The damp, Frito-scented air of the crowded stairwell has dissipated and been replaced by a cooler, fresher school smell of floor wax and urinal cakes. I've reached the third floor.

My locker is dead ahead, and I drag myself to it with my backpack and my dignity somehow still intact. All this just for the privilege of shedding a few eight-pound textbooks for the night. A stupid salmon who makes it all the way upstream at least gets to spawn. Lucky fish.

DORK!

A few minutes later, I'm leaning against the van, talking to my friend Tim, when my girlfriend, Sara, and her best friend, D'ijon, come dancing out of school. They're singing this ancient Katy Perry song (Note to all girls: This never gets old), and

after a final spin and a little
butt thrust, Sara throws
her arm around my neck
and kisses me on the
cheek. "Hi, Jeremy."

"Hey," I manage.

Let me just say this: Sara
Toomey is hot. She's not
Cheerleader Hot or Brazilian
Supermodel Hot . . . she's more
Ohio Hot. Perfect, okay, but not
airbrushed and with just a few minor flaws to make her majorly
interesting. She has this great smile (my dad was her orthodontist, so I guess I have him to partially thank for that) and
a dancer's body that just moves in all the right directions at all
the right times. But the best thing about Sara is the way she

talks. She's really, really smart, but she gets her words mixed up sometimes and comes up with more assaults on the English language than country music. Some of my recent favorites are:

I defy anyone to not fall in love with that.

I wipe the drool off my chin, and the four of us pile into the van. The girls scrunch way down in the back, afraid to be seen and ratted out to their parents. I guess they promised that they'd never ride in it for safety reasons or something, but I think it probably has as much to do with the lack of seat upholstery or possibly the exhaust fumes that waft up from the rusted floorboard under the front seat.

I finally find the key at the bottom of my backpack and wave my arm out the window to give the ignition signal. There's an electric snapping sound, a little yelp, and then the engine roars—okay, wheezes—to life. The passenger door flies

open and my amigo Hector Garcia hauls himself into shotgun.

"Hey," he says as he digs between the seat and the backrest for the seat belt.

"'Sup," I say, just because I feel chatty.

Hector is six foot six and pushing 230 pounds. We've been best friends since we were, like, four years old. We met on a dirt pile in front of the house that my mom and dad were building. That was where we discovered a common interest (dirt) and, even more important, that we were going to be in the same preschool class. It wasn't Best Friends at First Sight or anything with us. In fact, it wasn't until I bit Hector during a glue stick struggle and we had to spend an hour sharing our feelings about it with Miss Jenny that we became what you would call friends.

He rightfully bit me back after Miss Jenny let us go, making us even and launching an amigoship that's lasted all the way through elementary school and middle school.

We co-own the van, Hector and me, but he's the one who found a way to start the engine after the ignition switch got wonky. And he says that he hardly even feels the shocks anymore. However, I take credit for noticing that the wires on his retainer happen to be the perfect length for this operation. Since Hector always wears his retainer, he's the designated starter, and we're never without a van key. I'm happy, he's happy, and his orthodontist has a BMW.

Plus, the faint electrical-ozone tang on Hector's breath is an improvement over the smell of his grandma's habanero red sauce that he pours on almost everything he eats (I saw him put it on a bowl of Lucky Charms once, in case you think I'm exaggerating). The guy has a Kevlar stomach.

The van shudders forward like some kind of arctic Chihuahua as we inch along in the school parking lot traffic (I do the best I can, but we do need to get that clutch fixed). I don't know why the traffic is always so bad. You have maybe two or three hundred teen-age drivers who are all in an insane rush to get as far away from school as fast as possible. Could someone please explain it to me? The van rolls forward another quarter-tire revolution. We're moving slower than the line outside the women's restroom at a concert.

Speaking of concerts, Hector turns around and rests his meaty elbows on the back of the seat. He smiles at Sara and D'ijon as he scratches the little soul patch under his lower lip with two shiny Gingivitis passes. "I wonder if there's anybody we know who's cool enough to have actual tickets to the actual Gingivitis concert next weekend," he fake muses.

"OHMYGAWDICAN'TBELIEVEYOUGUYSGOTTICKETS," the girls scream.

The line of cars trying to get out of the school parking lot is endless, so we have plenty of time to really rub it in. So I say, "Gosh, if I knew you were interested, I would have gotten tickets for you— Oh, wait . . . you're the girls with curfews who always follow the rules."

"I am *so* jealous." Sara pouts as she grabs the tickets from Hector. She sniffs them and then starts rubbing them all over her neck. "Mmmmmm . . . ." she purrs. "I can almost smell the roadies!"

This is the effect that certain music has on females, and the main reason I have dedicated my life to rock music. It's common knowledge that the average rock star is up to 30 percent uglier than the average non–rock star, yet 900 percent more likely to be seen hanging out with supermodels. It's simple math.

D'ijon grabs the tickets from Sara and starts studying them like some kind of an exam guide before a midterm.

"Can you imagine what our parents would say if they saw us even *holding* these tickets?"

GASP!

See, Gingivitis has a reputation for some pretty insane stage behavior. Sure, there has been the occasional wardrobe slippage, virgin sacrifice, and live animal ingestion, but it's not like these guys use that to get attention. They are first and foremost musicians. And people always bring this up, but I personally think the exploding-porpoise-bazooka thing never really happened and was just some story their publicist concocted to sell tickets . . . which is something that I can't believe they even need to worry about.

SHOCK!

These guys are gods.

KABLOOOOEY!

Their music is the basis for everything our band is and wants to be. Seriously, Gingivitis is arguably the best guitar mayhem band since Flatulent Rat, and that's not something I would say casually.

Anyway, we're all talking while Tim (who's always quiet normally) just sits there watching it all happen and texting somebody off and on.

I look at Hector and say pretty loudly, "Dude, what kind of loser sells tickets to a Gingivitis concert when he's not having brain surgery or something?"

And Hector goes, "Unfathomable, dude."